HUNTER

THE FRACTURED FAIRYTALE SERIES

J. A. WYNTERS

Hunter

Editing by: Dear Jane Editing

Cover design: The Dust Jacket Designs

Interior Formatting: Dawn Lucous, Yours Truly Book Services

To the broken hearted

Hunter

There is something magical about weddings.

They bring the feral out of single girls. Like all the joy and happiness makes them miserable and drown in self-loathing, and all they need is a cock to make them feel special. Lucky for them tonight, that cock was going to be mine.

One of the bridesmaids has been making eyes at me throughout the whole ceremony and I've dropped enough smiles, winks and a few passing comments about her beautiful face to pretty much seal the deal.

I drink just enough to be in party mood and hope she's doing the same. Drunk girls are fun, paralytic ones are too much hard work, and I don't plan on working any more tonight than I have to. If Wolf was here, he'd give me one of his looks and another lecture about drinking on the job, the guy is all about keeping it professional, he's not wrong of course, and I do, but my shift is coming to an end and it's been another long week.

I look around the room at the uber-rich and socialites all trying to be better, prettier and more special than their counterparts. Turns out no matter how you dress them, people are all the same, attention starved and looking for something.

And I'm a good guy, always happy to make that *something* be me.

I scan the room for the hundredth time. No danger, nothing out of the ordinary, just another rich guy marrying a rich girl, they'll split up in a year or so and their faces will be splashed in all the tabloids as their marriage breaks apart and every indiscretion gets analysed. Lucky for me, I don't give a shit. It's not part of my work description.

I call Rob on the two-way radio, "Hey Rob, can you come take over? I'm clocking off for the night."

"On my way." His voice crackles into the radio and my eyes sweep the room. The petite brunette is standing next to a friend. They're both wearing bridesmaids' dresses, and all I can see is ass and tits as they spill from the horrendous peach fabric. I can't wait to get her out of that dress. Really, I'll be doing her a favour.

I catch her eye, step off my podium and flash her a smile. Even from this distance I notice the way her eyes grow round, and her smile stretches, she whispers something to her friend and they both look at me. Hungry like. My cock twitches in my pants and I start walking towards the exit. When I look back, the brunette has linked an arm with her friend and they're both walking in my direction. I turn back to Rob and tell him I'll see him at the office tomorrow. He follows my gaze; it locks on the two women crossing the room. I notice the slight shift of his posture and the minute ghost of a smile before he nods. I turn to walk towards the exit which connects the hotel lobby to the elevator bank.

I lean against the wall and wait for the two girls to emerge. They walk out of the ballroom and eye me. One's eyes are hungry and wild, the other has a nervous smile plastered across her face.

"Hi," I say all casual like even though my cock is about to burst out of my pants.

"Hey," the brunette one takes the lead, her friend just keeps smiling as if it's going to save her from me.

"Would you mind if my friend joins us?"

I look her up and down—blonde hair, tight as fuck body, perky little tits, and full glistening lips. Of course, I don't fucking mind. "Not at all." I flash her a smile.

Brunette presses the elevator button, and it pings. We get in and she pushes number five. The air is thick in here, anticipation, nervousness, excitement. If it wasn't for all the cameras everywhere, I would have already launched myself at them.

"What's your name?" I ask and zero on the friend. She's pretty and shy, her cheeks are flushed with pink, and she keeps chewing on her lower lip.

"Ava." She whispers and looks down. Everything inside me erupts in a hot surging fire. Having that inhibited little mouth wrapped around my cock is going to be sensational.

"I'm Isi." The brunette drawls, taking charge. "What's your name?"

"Liam." It's not. But she doesn't need to know my real name or anything else about me. If I've learned anything seeing Wolf all shot up, it's the less people know about you, the better.

The elevator is thrown open and Isi rushes out pulling Ava behind her. There's something damn sexy about a shy girl—like she's hiding a secret, but you know that when she opens up and tells you about it, it's going to be crazy and wild. My body tenses at the thought.

Isi grabs the keycard and unlocks her room door, holding

it open for us. I follow Ava inside, my eyes locked on her tight, little ass.

"Would you like a drink?" Isi offers from somewhere behind me.

I shrug, "sure." Whatever they need to get the edge off, followed by their dresses.

I sink into the couch and Isi offers me a beer. It's cold and bitter and I only half listen to the conversation. My gaze keeps being drawn to Ava and the way she keeps dragging her teeth over her lower lip. I'm questioning why we're all still dressed when Isi mounts my thighs and slides down till she rolls over my cock and my hands automatically lock around her ass.

She's lovely, if overeager. I don't mind, I like a sure thing. But I also like to unwrap a mystery. Unlocking Ava will feel like completing the boss level in a video game. I can't fucking wait to conquer her.

Isi's mouth is on mine and her tongue slips past the seam of my lips. She tastes like the cranberry that she threw into her vodka, but I know the kind of girl she is, that's the only sweet thing about her. She slips her hands into my hair and rakes her finger over my scalp, rolling her hips over my hardening erection. She rips off my clip-on tie and begins to unbutton my dress shirt, slipping her hands onto my skin and running her nails along my ribs.

I grip her zip and slide it down her back. Her dress falls open and pools between us. Ava watches us, her gaze follows our hands and mouths, her breathing quickens, the blush of her cheeks intensifies. She steps closer to us and her hands slide along Isi's back while she kisses me again. Ava's delicate hands unclasp Isi's bra and her breasts spill out, and my hands instinctively reach over to cup them. She arches into me and stretches herself reaching for Ava.

I can't help but groan when their lips touch. Isi's sure moves, Ava's uncertain exploration. It's fucking breathtaking.

When they break away Ava's eyes remain on mine and her voice wavers, "Can we go to the room?"

Isi flashes her a smile and climbs off me, "sure." She takes Ava by the hand and leads her to the bedroom.

When I get there, they are sitting on the perfectly made bed of crispy white sheets. Isi turns to Ava and kisses her. She's eager and hungry, while Ava is still timid. She holds back like a flower in moonlight, but I know that—when she eventually relents—she'll bloom and she'll be so fucking beautiful. My cock pulses against my pants and I suck in long deep breaths reminding myself I have all night.

The kiss gets hungrier and deeper as Isi pushes Ava onto the bed, her knee tucked between her legs. A groan escapes as her tongue twists with Ava's.

Her mouth travels down to her neck and shoulders. Ava isn't relaxed, not yet; she's still tense, her eyes on me, her cheeks a deep, beautiful crimson.

"Let's get this off," Isi says as she pulls Ava up and slowly unzips the dress, pulling it down her lithe body.

Ava isn't wearing a bra and I'm staring at the most perfect pair of tits I've ever seen—round and soft with shell-pink nipples, peaked at the ready. She bites her lower lip, sucking it in as she watches Isi pull off her thong and toss it aside.

Isi crawls back onto the bed, her tongue flickers out and she runs it along Ava's pale skin leaving a long glistening trail behind. She tongues her breasts, licking and nuzzling the white mounds and sucking her nipples. Ava throws her head back and moans, her nervousness falling away, evaporating as her friend explores her body.

My eyes remain glued to the two women on the bed as I undo my pants and pull them down.

"Come join us," Isi mewls and Ava turns pink again, the colour sweeping across her face and breasts. Fuck, she looks delectable.

"I will, but for now I'm enjoying the show."

Isi licks her lips as if I've somehow challenged her and her mouth closes on her friend's tits, sucking and licking, her nipples pebbling when they meet the cool air. Kissing down her stomach, she lowers herself between Ava's legs. Ava's eyes flicker open and lock onto mine. I'm standing over the bed stroking my cock watching Isi's tongue torment her friend. Fuck it's hot and beautiful and I'm so hard it's excruciating to keep holding back.

Ava moans, her perky tits shake and move as her hips gyrate against Isi's face. Her small body shakes, her face contorts and she reaches for the headboard clutching it, white bleeding into her knuckles as a desperate savage moan rips from her mouth. Her whimpers keep going as waves of intense release wash over her, and she rocks her hips against Isi's mouth until every last tremor is complete.

I grab Isi and kiss her deep, wanting to taste Ava on her tongue. I'm rewarded by the salty-sweet flavour that coats Isi's mouth and tongue. Isi's kiss is hunger and desire but when I've had my taste, I cast her aside and reach for Ava. I close my mouth over hers and she opens up for me desperately. Her hands tug my hair, and she pulls me to her like she's still falling and she needs something to cling onto. I'm more than happy to be that something.

"Would you like some help with that?" Isi stares at my throbbing cock.

I flash her smile saying nothing and stand back up to my full height. She shuffles to the edge of the bed, grips my cock and sucks me inside. A guttural, savage groan spills from somewhere inside me. Her mouth is so hot, expertly gliding up and down.

Isi unlatches with a satisfied smile. "Your turn," she says to Ava, who giggles.

She looks up at me as if asking permission and I think I might explode with those big, wondering eyes and exquisite fucking body. She leans in and licks the tip of my cock and strokes my balls, sending shivers down my spine.

"Oh fuck," I choke out as she takes me deeper, her hands stroking everywhere her mouth can't be.

When she unlatches, I think I might fall apart. But Isi is there instead, moaning as she sucks me in, sending me spiraling.

My breaths get shorter, rougher, more demanding, and she takes me deeper. I sink my hands into Isi's hair just as Ava takes over again.

My senses reel as they double down, take turns, push me close, then pull away. Their hands are everywhere on my shaft and my balls. Two sets of tongues lick and their hot mouths suck and dive, taking me deeper each time. I grab Ava's perfect breast and roll my finger over her hard nipple, her moan is almost enough to set me over the edge. My grip tightens in Isi's hair and I grunt, fucking her mouth, desperate now. Everything tightens and for a split second, I feel lightheaded as I growl and come hard and fast into the back of Isi's throat.

The girls fall back onto the bed and I fall with them.

"What about me?" Isi pouts.

I drag her over and kiss her, then make my way down her body. My tongue flicks over her clit and she moans, and as I look up her body, I find myself staring at Ava. Her pink lips close over her friend's nipples and her tongue swirling over the tight pink flesh, her teeth dragging it out while her hands explore. Isi grinds against my mouth, her orgasm mounting. I insert a finger inside her, then a second. Ava bites down and Isi explodes, a shattering moan has her body shivering and her breath broken and my cock hard and ready to go.

I reach for Ava and kiss her. Her hungry, delicious mouth is eager, and my hands touch all her curves, relishing the feel of her. I lie on my back and she straddles me. She's so fucking tight and so fucking hot, I groan at the feel of her as she slides up and down my shaft, working her hips.

Isi comes behind her, playing with her breasts, pinching her nipples then sliding down to her clit. I groan at the sight of Ava's sweaty body being played with. I thrust deeper, pleasure building inside me like a torrent as her own pleasure builds.

We are a flurry of skin, lips, tongues and cock. Her rhythm speeds up, her hips smash against mine, her breathing comes out in sharp short moans and whimpers, before her pussy clenches so tightly around my cock and she cries out her pleasure. I thrust a final time and come so fucking hard I think I might pass out for a second. Her pussy clenches and tightens and pleasure smashes through me.

I fall back into the bed and suck in air. The girls giggle in delight around me, hands roaming my naked body, the bed smelling of sex and lavender body lotion and goddam I love my fucking job.

2

Hunter

The beginnings of a headache scratch at my skull, and my foul mood is about to take a turn for the worse. I stare at the computer screen, thirty new emails in the last two hours, endless paperwork and deluded rich assholes who require our services.

I'm busy reading over one from a recluse on an island who wants a guard to come live with him full time when Rob walks in.

"You look like shit." He announces to the room.

"That's not what you said last night when you spooned me and told me you loved me."

"We both know I'll say anything to get you on your knees."

I scoff, "Keep dreaming. I was up all night fucking your mum."

"If you were fucking my mum, you'd look worse. That woman will break you." We both chuckle and grimace at the image. "What's up? Didn't get your cock sucked like you like last night?"

"Nah, your mum kept her teeth in."

"That explains a lot."

I shrug.

Rob walks over to the fridge and pulls out some bottled water. "I have to say, I am surprised though. I saw you exchange looks with some chick all night."

I nod. *Some chick.* "Yeah, she was hot as fuck. I was sure she was into it, but it turns out I was wasting my time."

"What happened?"

"You know, I gave her the look, she flashed me a bunch of smiles, flicked her hair, gave me all the signals. The more the night went on the more she played up. And then I realised who she was," I push back from my desk and lean back into my chair. "Do you remember Olivia?"

His eyes narrow and scratches his chin before recognition has him opening his mouth, "*The* Olivia? The one Wolf was desperate to bang and chased around like a puppy every chance he got?"

"Yeah, her." I chuckle. Wolf was almost as desperate for her as he was for my sister. He came close a few times, but Olivia kept turning him down. She was one of the rare few who got away from him, and I know that even if he won't admit it, he still thinks about it sometimes.

"Oh her. Is she still hot?"

I nod. She is, but she's a bit more than that. I shrug. "Anyway, we were getting ready to wrap up and she had her eye on me. She was radiating need. That woman wanted me, and man, I was ready to take her upstairs and fuck her senseless. But as I'm walking up to her, some guy comes out of nowhere, wraps his arm around her, and starts kissing her." I grind my teeth, agitation slithering up my neck. What a fucking waste of time. "I just stood there like an idiot as she walked by me with him all over her. What a fucking tease."

Rob wears an amused look and I want to wipe it off his face, but I'm too tired. "Who cares, she's just another chick, hundreds like her everywhere."

I shrug, he's technically right, "This is true. However, if I'd had her, I would have made sure to let Wolf know, and I'd never let him live it down."

At that, Rob bursts out laughing and shakes his head. He gets it. "When is he back?"

I look at the calendar on the wall, "A few more weeks." I sigh.

He's taken Red away to Croatia. Ever since getting shot and shacking up with my sister, he's discovered this newfound love for life. He suddenly has one. And he's happy. He deserves to be, and I like that he makes Red happy too.

After so many months of living in a hotel room and working around the clock to keep everything ticking along while Wolf has been recovering, it's been great getting back to business as usual. With Jenny behind bars and all our names cleared, I'm looking forward to my right-hand man being back. After all, he's not just my business partner, he's also my best mate. Rob is a good number two, but he's no Wolf.

Rob drags a chair over to my desk; it scraps the floor like nails on chalk and he shoots me a 'fuck you' smile as I cringe at the sound. He'll pay for that later. We go over the schedule for the next few weeks, double-checking clients and manpower. We'll need to do another recruitment drive soon. I roll my eyes. I'll set Wolf on that when he gets back, sucking some of his newfound happiness away. It's making him soft.

I read through my emails, answer clients and consolidate accounts, my eyes burn by the time I'm done. I check my watch; I have about an hour's worth of work left and then I can go home and have a nap before another gig tonight.

I've been working too many shifts lately. My body feels it; not enough sleep, interrupted meals and no routine of any sort. I could easily take a break—I am part owner of our security business—but I don't.

Every night there are different challenges and many, many rewards. A few fights to break up with minuscule men with Napoleon complexes and too much alcohol in their systems, and desperate women who are more than eager to go with me to the toilet and make me happy. They want to see me smile from their knees, and I'm not one to deny a beautiful lady what she wants. I'm selfless like that.

Rob's voice drones on about something and the words on the screen blur when my phone rings. I don't recognise the number and frown.

"Hello?"

"Mr. Evans?" A sweet female voice has me automatically on edge. Very few women have my private number and I know exactly who they are.

"Who wants to know?"

"This is Emily Shepard, Daryl Dark's personal assistant."

Daryl Dark, a frikking legend in the rock scene, the man has been around longer than the pope, he's been around every fucking block—twice—and his reputation precedes him. The name Dark suits him from what I hear, his clothes, his lyrics, his attitude and the way his PA is ruining my already shitty mood. "How did you get this number?"

"It was personally given to me by Mr. Dark. He said it was passed on by a certain musician who says he owes you his life."

I nod into the phone. That could be a number of people. I set the thought aside, for now, intrigued, despite my better judgement. "What can I do for you, Miss Shepard?"

"It's Emily," she clarifies as if it's an important detail, "Mr. Dark is coming to London next week. He plans on renting property for at least six weeks while he records his new album. He'll require some personal protection while in town."

"So, why are you calling me?"

"He requires your services." Her voice is curt and lathered with condescension.

"Where are his usual guys?"

"A few will accompany us to London, but he would prefer a local, someone who knows the territory and knows what's going on. You've come more than highly recommended."

I rub my hand across my chin and look at our current client list and upcoming events. With a bit of juggling and overtime, I guess we can squeeze in one more client. It's a short-term contract and if I send Rob, I can cover his shifts till Wolf gets back.

"I'll brief one of my guys and have him contact you, just sen—"

"No. Mr. Dark wants you to do it." Her rudeness is starting to rub me the wrong way and I'm tempted to hang up.

"Look, Miss Shepard, I—"

"It's Emily and Daryl wants you."

I sigh. This is already too difficult. "Let me see what I can do."

"Fantastic, I knew he could count on you."

"I didn't s—" but she hangs up before I can finish. I grind my teeth and glare at my phone. "What the fuck?!"

Rob looks up at me and raises an eyebrow.

"Just some asshole who thinks I'll ask how high when he tells me to jump. Don't need that kind of headache." But even as I finish talking, determined to let Mr. Dark sort out his own shit without me, my phone rings again and I see a familiar name on the screen.

I suck in a galvanising breath and swipe, bringing it to my ear. "Mr. Legend, it's been a long time." *Not long enough.* My head falls back into my chair and I glare at the ceiling, why does this day keep shitting on me?

"I told you to call me Justin."

"Yeah, you did. What can I do for you?"

"I believe a mutual friend got in touch?"

"Well, his pushy PA did. Look, I don't thi—"

"I was hoping to speak to you before she got in touch but Daryl likes to jump the gun."

"You don't say." I roll my eyes.

He chuckles on the other end. "Look, you'll be doing me a *personal* favour, I'll owe you one."

My grip tightens around my phone and I exhale sharply. "I'll see what I can do."

"Thank you."

"Sure." We both know I don't mean it. I hang up, shove my phone into my back pocket and grab my keys. An email drops in from Mr. Dark's personal assistant with all the details for Daryl Dark's impending visit. I leave it unread and head for the door.

Rob eyes me again, "So, how high you gonna jump boss?"

"High enough to teabag your mum." I snap at him and stomp out of the office, his laughter echoes in my wake.

3

Hunter

aryl Dark is the epitome of your stereotypical rock star. He had a wild history and is often a headliner in music magazines. He's more famous for his infamy than his illustrious rock career, but any which way you look at him, the man is a musical genius and a survivor. In a sea full of fish, he became a shark. He was always ahead of everyone else, smashing out hit after hit after hit. It's part of the reason his record company pays to cover shit up and buys stories from the editor's desk before they hit the tabloids. All in all, the man was a walking arrogant dick that thought the world owed him something and he is currently strolling towards me.

I steel myself. This is going to suck.

He waves at no one and smiles at invisible fans. I shake my head already picturing the delusions and paranoia he's just offloaded from his private jet. A leather jacket is flung over his shoulder and he's wearing a dangerously faded pair of denim that look like they're staying intact by sheer will power.

He reaches the Audi and extends a thin, muscular corded arm, covered in faded black tattoos that have bleached and bled into the skin over the years. He has young, icy-blue eyes set in an aging man's face, his forehead mapped with deep lines and crow's feet.

"You're the guy?" he asks in a deep Liverpudlian accent.

I shrug, "Hunter. Good to meet you, Mr. Dark."

"Of course it is." He winks at me and shoves a bag into my hands before stepping towards the car. He stops, his body halfway inside, then looks up the tarmac towards the noisy jet, "Hurry up now, love. We don't have all fucking day, now do we?" he shouts then disappears into the Audi.

I follow his gaze. A woman hurries towards us. She's pulling one of those suitcases on wheels, one seems to be broken and it wiggles around as she struggles to catch up. She is as drab and enthusiastic as the tarmac. A grey suit, crisp white shirt, shiny white shoes designed for comfort and efficiency over style, a too-tight bun and a face set so firmly, she looks like a walking mannequin. She reaches the car and gives me a cold smile that's as genuine as a car salesman, ditches her suitcase and slips into the car without a word. My whole face tightens and my jaw clamps.

Emily Shepard. The PA. Rob did the regular checks on her knowing she would accompany Mr. Dark. Unfortunately, he found nothing out of the ordinary. The only daughter of Mr. and Mrs. Shepard, graduated top of her class from the University of Birmingham. Did a few odd jobs before landing this role. She's been Daryl's PA for two years and she looks as if it's worn her down. If my memory serves, she's meant to be twenty-five, but dresses like a seventy-year-old at her mother's funeral. I guess her dress sense matches her personality. Cold and drab. I shrug. Not my problem anyway.

"Let me get that for you," I mumble to myself as I pass the bags to Tom, the driver, to load into the boot before I get into the passenger side of the car.

I give Tom the go ahead and we pull away and towards the apartment Mr. Dark had rented for his visit. Tom has already been briefed on the route we are taking and the entry point into the house.

A funky smell derails my thoughts and I look back to see Daryl inhale a lungful of his foul-smelling cigarette. The ember burns a bright orange before a river of smoke cascades from his mouth and spills into the car.

"This is a non-smoking vehicle, sir." I try for polite while opening all the windows to let the stench out.

"Sure it is." He replies and puts the cigarette to his mouth again. The woman sitting next to him squirms uncomfortably, her face turned away.

"I have to insist you put that out, sir."

"It's just a smoke, guy, take it easy."

I instruct Tom to pull over as I grit my teeth and grip my chair. Everyone has to die sometimes right? "Sir put the cigarette out now."

He takes another drag as if I don't even register on his radar, his eyes lock on mine for a second before he blows out the smoke and chucks the cigarette out the window. He falls back into his seat, his arms crossed like a petulant teenager.

I turn and face the front again and motion for the driver to continue. I suck in shallow breaths, knowing the fucking smell will linger in the upholstery. Something about cigarette smoke, it sinks into everything. Every hair, every cotton fiber — even skin—like it's petrified to vanish.

Damn it! My clothes smell like they've been worn by an old tramp, and even with the windows down the tincture of cigarette fumes clings to my nose.

By the time we pull into the driveway, I've regained some composure and pushed my anger aside, remembering the pay cheque at the end of this deep, long, dark tunnel which is Daryl Dark.

I accompany him into the mansion. It is a world unto itself. People who do not have exuberant amounts of money at their disposal have no real understanding of how the other half lives. This humble abode, as he called it, was like a life-size representation of Daryl Dark's ego designed out of bricks and mortar. Overly large and ostentatious with all the trimmings.

He scans the place and turns to Emily. "Where the fuck are my guitars?"

"Waiting at the studio."

"All of them?" his face tightens.

"Yes." Her voice shrinks a little and I fight the urge not to stand between them.

"What the fuck good is that to me if all my guitars are there and I'm here?"

"Well, you said… I thought—"

"Thinking doesn't suit you, love, and you should do less of it!" He huffs, "I'm going to shower, that should give you enough time to get Raven and Black Dust over here." He doesn't wait for an answer before he stomps away and into the house.

The way he talks to her has the muscles in my back bunched up. She might be a cold, irritating, know-it-all, but everyone deserves a modicum of respect.

She avoids my eyes before grabbing her phone. "Hi Tom, can you bring the car around?" She holds for a beat before dashing to the door, her shoes silent on the tiles. "Great, I'll be right out." She disappears outside, and a car door slams.

I shake my head. *What the fuck was that?* I pull out my phone and dial Justin. He picks up after the second ring.

"Mr. Legend," I start.

"It's Justin." He corrects me again knowing I'll never call him by his first name.

"I think you need to find someone else to do this job."

"It's only been a few hours."

"A few hours too long." The tension building in my back grips and tightens.

"There's no one else." He states.

"Have you tried anyone else?"

"No. No one else can do his job but you."

"I don't think I can either."

There's a short silence before he speaks again, "I'll owe you one, and I'll pay double what you usually charge for services."

"It's not a money thing."

"It's always a money thing, everyone has a price."

"Why is this so important to you?"

There's a long exhale on the other end of the line. "It's personal. I need this favour."

"And I'm it?"

The silence from the other end is enough of an answer.

"The man is a dick."

"He's worse than that." Justin chuckles. "Thanks, Hunter, I know I can count on you." He hangs up before I have a chance to say anything more.

I tuck the phone back into my back pocket and grind my teeth wishing for the first time ever I was sitting outside on a stool at some dodgy club dealing with drunk fucks.

4

Emily

I slam the door to the car a little more violently than I mean to and Tom takes off without a word. My heart sits somewhere in my throat clogging the scream I want to release. Fucking Daryl. I hate it when he speaks to me so dismissively and I hate the way I still react to him after all these years. I know he's nothing but a man-child that needs to be constantly watched so that he doesn't hurt himself, but his brash words and his attitude still sting.

The thing that irks me most is that he knows who I am, and it's like he's trying to coax a reaction out of me. Force me to do something other than my submissive responses and annoyed replies. Whatever his motives are, I suspect they have nothing to do with me and everything to do with *him*. I can't wait to break away from both of them and breathe on my own.

I draw in another breath and promise myself that the next eight months would be my last. I ignore the stupid voice in my head that tries to remind me I've been saying that for the last two years. Instead, I allow my anger to keep simmering while I think about the meathead who stood next to Daryl and looked at me like I needed saving—like I was helpless.

Hunter Evans. His piercing green eyes stared at me as Daryl snapped his fingers. I huff pretending I didn't notice the sharp angle of his jaw or his muscular forearms. Just another idiot with a hero complex. A good looking one, but still an idiot.

I stare out of the window and remember how much I hate London. Being back here feels like walking through an endless memory. One I hoped I'd put behind me. Every time I come back here I know it should feel like home, instead, it just feels empty.

I watch the buildings drift by in blurs and look up to the familiar grey sky, as much as I want to hate it, it fills me with nostalgia.

Tom pulls up at the studio and I climb out of the car waiting for the day I'd be here as more than just someone's PA.

5

Hunter

I look at my watch. It's exactly 9 a.m.–the time Emily informed me that Daryl wanted to leave just before I departed last night. My shirt is already wet with sweat and clings to my body, feeling too tight around my throat as I stand outside like an idiot. After ten minutes, I knock. Keeping my temper in check and not kicking the fucking door off its hinges.

It opens and Emily stands on the other side. She's in another grey suit only slightly lighter than the day before, her hair is strung as tight as she is. She doesn't smile. "He'll be running late; you might as well get used to it."

"Great." I grind out and the sun's heat pushes against me. It's still early but it's going to be a hot day. Why anyone would record an album during the few weeks of a British summer is beyond me.

"We're not leaving before eleven at the earliest." She's polite and curt and hides halfway behind the door like she might be afraid that I bite. She looks at the floor and her teeth graze over her lower lip before her gaze swings back to my face, hers indifferent. "Would you like to wait inside?"

I run a hand over my face, it's too hot, "sure, thanks."

I step inside and she's already halfway across the room as if she's running away from me. I close the door behind me and follow her through the foyer that's almost the size of my entire house, before veering left and into an exquisite modern kitchen.

It strikes me how white and clean it is. It's the opposite of mine. Especially since Wolf's special paint job before he left and took Red with him. I set that problem aside considering for the hundredth time if I should get another roommate or rent the place out and get something smaller just for me. I promise myself to deal with it after this job, just like I did after the last one.

"How do you take your coffee?" She asks, looking at the mug in her hands.

"Very seriously." I deadpan. Her mouth doesn't move an inch. *Ice queen.* When she doesn't respond at all, I ask for a splash of milk and one sugar. She makes the coffee and sets the mug in front of me.

"Thank you."

She throws me a half fake smile and looks away before rounding the table to sit across from me. A stack of papers spread out in front of her as she clicks on a laptop and focuses on the screen. If I didn't know any better, I'd think she was putting a barrier between us. Not that she needs one.

It gives me a chance to study her. She's perched on top of the stool with her legs crossed and sits upright. I can tell she has a small frame but it's swallowed in the stupid grey suit that doesn't compliment her complexion at all. It's like she is trying to disappear. Her hazel eyes are hidden behind glasses, and her make-up is natural and sparse. There's something about her, but whatever it is she is trying to hide it and her personality is as dull as her suits. I wonder if that's why he hired her. All business and no play. She will definitely make Hunter a dull boy.

I sip on my coffee and take a few minutes to look through my phone and check emails. Red has tried to tag Wolf again in some Instagram story, and the picture is blurred as his face moves out of the frame. I shake my head, my face splitting in an amused grin. Eventually she'll learn the man doesn't like his picture taken. Until then, it's another blurred photo for her growing collection. I answer a few emails and put my phone away knowing Rob will take care of things.

"I'm Hunter by the way. We spoke on the phone."

She startles by the sound of my voice and jumps a little. I snicker and pink bleeds into her cheeks. "Emily. I know who you are." She doesn't look at me.

"I feel like we might have started on the wrong foot," I'm not sure why I'm extending this olive branch, she's a cold, boring, snappy, bossy, rude little thing, but experience has taught me that jobs go much smoother if everyone gets along. Or at least if someone offers you a decent cup of coffee in the morning.

"Did we?"

Her cold demeanour has my back up, "I um—"

Daryl strolls into the kitchen in a pair of boxers and nothing else and saves me from a conversation she's clearly not interested in having. Emily's posture changes immediately, her face tightens and her whole body looks like it's been filled with cement, it's rigid and taut.

"Coffee!" he snaps his fingers, and she jumps off the stool to make his cup. Irritation prickles my skin. I don't like the way he talks to her.

He stands in the middle of the kitchen with a hand down his pants and his long bottled black hair tumbling down his back. I wonder what the press would make of it if he had a fatal fall in his kitchen.

She hands him his coffee and he doesn't say a thing before walking out of the kitchen.

"Does he always speak to you that way?" I ask, my hands tightening around my mug.

"It's fine." She avoids my eyeline and rushes to her paperwork gathering it all up and looking anywhere but at me.

I grind my teeth as I watch her. "Thanks for the coffee," I place my half-drunk cup in the sink. "I'll wait outside."

She nods—barely—and I leave her with her paperwork and rosy cheeks.

***

Emily

I watch him march out of the room and a little flutter passes through me. It's not like I need him to get angry on my behalf, but for some reason his reaction sparks something inside me that has me feeling something other than irritation. Of course, it helps that his jeans grip onto his ass like their life depends on it, and even when angry, he exudes sex appeal.

I feel a little guilty at my coldness towards him, he was trying to be nice and I was trying to remain invisible little Emily Shepard, that keeps her head down and her secrets buried. Hunter has the kind of face that makes girls do stupid things they regret in the morning, and I have plans that can't be derailed by green eyes, bulging muscles and a sexy smile that tilts a little more to the left.

I allow a little smile to creep up to my lips as I think about his stupid coffee joke then wipe it away as I look over at the stash of paperwork.

I sigh, getting ready to resume my seat where I can hurry up and wait for Daryl.

My phone rings and I swipe before thinking.

"Hi, Darling."

"Hello, father."

"Oh don't do that darling."

"Do what?"

He sighs and moves on. "How's work?" he sounds as condescending as ever.

"You know how it is."

"Yes well, we both know how Daryl can be."

I say nothing. And a strange yet familiar silence hangs between us. "Was there a reason you called?"

"You're in London, I thought maybe you'd want to drop in?"

I inhale the last bit of the air in the kitchen then exhale very slowly, "I'm really busy with work and..."

"I've told you before, you don't have to keep working for him, I can open any door for you."

"I want to open my own doors."

I can sense him nodding as I speak. "Just like your mother."

"Don't talk about her."

We're back to silence but it's gone from familiar to uncomfortable. Or maybe that's how it always is, it's just easier to notice when I'm angry. And lately, I'm always angry.

Except just before, when Hunter made me smile. I brush away the thought, "I have to go."

"Think about my offer darling."

"I will." I won't. "Bye."

I hang up before he calls me darling again and stare at the stack of papers on the breakfast table. Contracts I'll be spending all day trying to get Daryl to sign. I sigh and look at the collection of framed pictures hanging in the foyer. Hall of Famers that I assume have stayed in this house previously. I know all their names and at least one song from each of their albums, in fact, I've met most of them. As I turn away I make a silent vow to have my picture up there one day too.

I make another cup of coffee and Hunter's comment of it being very serious keeps floating around my head, I let the smile that keeps wanting to burst from me stay on my face. But only for a minute.

6

Hunter

We leave after mid-day and every nerve in my body is on edge. I can breathe as deep and as often as I like, but there is no calming me around this guy. It's been twenty-four hours and I'm about ready to throw him to the wolves.

I stare out of the window tracking every car and checking every street corner as we make our way to the studio. I know there's no need, but it's habit. I'm always looking over my shoulder. Tom takes the route we previously discussed and with the light afternoon traffic, we make good time.

We park in the underground parking and I follow Daryl into the studio, which I already know is secure, with only the producer waiting inside. They shake hands like old friends but as Daryl grabs his guitars, I see the eye roll. I bite down my smirk. Guess I'm not the only one pretending around his guy.

It's not the first time I've seen a musician create. But Daryl, despite his abrasive personality, really is a musical genius and though I thought I'd stand around all day with my dick in my hands watching just another guy with a guitar do his thing, Daryl lives up to his reputation. The man is a visionary.

A cigarette hangs from his mouth and smoke swirls in the booth as his fingers dance over the aged guitar. He'd recorded all his newer albums with her, his famed "Black Dust," and the older she gets, the more tonal she becomes. His fingers grip her wooden waist and when he plays her, he bleeds sound from her. It's like watching two lovers speak a language only they can understand.

He sits on the stool and from mere sounds, he throws out melodies and scribbles lyrics on a scruffy piece of paper he keeps in his back pocket. It seems that he reserves all his beauty for his art, and it all gets left behind in the small recording studio as soon as he steps out.

A few hours into recording he growls into the mic and sets his guitar aside. "This is shite mate," he calls out to the producer, who like me, clearly disagrees.

"What about a break Daryl?"

"Yeah, good idea." He tucks a long strand of hair behind his ear and grabs the mic. "Oi, Love." I follow his eyeline to find Emily sitting at the back of the room. She'd somehow managed to blend into the furniture.

She looks up from her laptop, looking like a deer in head-lights with an eighteen-wheeler coming her way.

"Coffee, and a sandwich, and be quick about it yeah?" he calls out and everyone's eyes fall away but mine. She tips her head and digs under her chair for a handbag which she throws over her shoulder. She walks over to where my body is blocking the door and lifts her eyes to mine. The hazel burns behind glistening eyes and I shoot Daryl an annoyed look, but he's too busy strumming his guitar to notice.

"Excuse me." She whispers and her eyes fall away.

I step aside and let her walk by me, her elbow grazes my

side as she passes but she doesn't look back at me, she rushes outside and vanishes around a corner.

I bite my tongue and say nothing, while the producer and Daryl talk over the last track he'd recorded and the changes he wants made. I zone out till my radio comes to life and one of the boys sitting outside lets me know Emily is on her way back inside.

I open the door just as she steps into the doorway. Her eyes meet mine and she hands me a wrapped-up sandwich and a plastic takeaway cup, "A splash of milk and one sugar right?"

I nod and accept the food from her as my brow furrows. My fingers brush over hers for just a second as I take the coffee cup and her eyes dart to mine and it looks like she might want to say something. She doesn't. She tears herself away and walks into the studio. Maybe that was her way of extending an olive branch. My stomach growls in appreciation as I watch her.

She hands out the rest of the food then goes to sit down at her desk again trying to disappear into the wall. She unwraps her own sandwich and takes a delicate bite. She covers her mouth with her hand like she's too afraid to be seen. The tips of her fingers touch her lips, and I can't help but stare. She has lovely lips. A little pouty, full and pink, I wonder how they might look locked around my cock.

I rip my eyes away and shake my head at the thought. No, I actually don't. I concentrate on my own sandwich and ignore her for the rest of the day which stretches well into the night. My shift should have ended hours ago, but Daryl's timetable doesn't conform to the hours he'd put down on paper. We will have to have words about that.

By the time we're back in the car, I can feel exhaustion creeping up on me. I grip the back of my neck and let my head fall on the headrest while Tom drives us back.

In the back Daryl is on his phone, "yeah brother, just got

into town," he pauses. "Sure, you should come over. Tell Dexter too."

Come over? I rub my eyes and think about the conversation I will need to have with this man in the morning about protocol and background checks and schedules. But as we pull into the driveway another car arrives. The hairs on the back of my neck stand to attention and before I can say two words to Daryl he is out of the car and heading towards the headlights. I jump out after him and close the distance in three strides then grab his elbow and pull him behind me.

"Let go." He says and tries to pry his arm out of my grip. He can try all he wants; he's not going anywhere.

"Mr. Dark," I exhale sharply, "I can't protect you if you don't let me. You can't just run off and—"

"Relax, it's just a few mates coming for a nightcap." He taps my hand like I'm a kid and my head wants to explode.

"Mr. Dark—" I'm cut off by approaching bodies and I automatically spin. The three men walking towards us all wear similar outfits and smiles. Torn up faded metal shirts, worn-out tired jeans and long black hair.

They approach Daryl who sidesteps me and they hug, then he leads them towards the house just as another car pulls into the driveway.

He turns back to me as the other three make their way inside. "Hey, I know I can be hard to work for, and maybe we started on the wrong foot, but it's been a long day, come in, have a drink with us. We'll sort the rest out in the morning yeah?"

"Mr. Dark—"

"Come," he puts his hand on my back and tries to move me. I relent and step towards the house just as I hear a third car pulling in.

The promised *"chilled"* explodes into a full-blown party in less than an hour. I'm not even sure where half of these people came from or who they are, but I'm technically off the clock so I allow myself to relax. A little. I know I'll be hearing all about this in the morning. Not to mention the angry and jealous glares from the boys standing around and working their shift, is making me feel just a little guilty. But only a little.

If Wolf was here he'd tear me a new one and give me his speech about keeping business and pleasure separate, except that he is the master of fucking up that cocktail. Or at least he used to be.

Dark is surrounded by beautiful women who throw themselves at him like glitter. The thing about glitter? It goes everywhere and sticks to everything. Even to me, it seems, as he sends a few my way. Maybe it's his way of apologising. I decide not to think about it too long or too hard as four women clad in tiny bikinis wrap themselves around me and drag me towards the house.

These poor, misguided groupies obviously came here looking for something, and I wasn't about to disappoint them—after all, I 'm the guy that's always happy being that something. As we make our way to a spare room they giggle and hop around all giddy, and my cock is ready to suck all that energy out of each and every one of them.

But just as we cross to the room, I spot Emily. Her eyes are on me, her mouth stretched in a thin line, and her hands are wrung together in front of her. I flash her a smile. She shakes her head and walks away.

"Whatever," I whisper to myself.

The door closes, shutting her judgement outside. I launch myself on my awaiting harem. These girls obviously need something right now, and I'm about to give it to them.

Fuck, I love my job. Sometimes.

7

Emily

I don't know why I am disappointed to see him close that door; I knew what he was the second I saw him. So what if he looked at me twice and said thank you, and made a swarm of butterflies take flight in my belly? I shake my head and keep staring at the door like I really expect him to change his mind and not fuck those four women. I grit my teeth at the image of a naked Hunter Evans and my stomach somersaults.

I tear my gaze from the door and march down the hall-way. Fuck this! Some of us still have work to do. That's not entirely true, not at 2 a.m. on a Wednesday morning, but seeing as I'm not going to put on a bikini and let any of those assholes touch me, I guess now is as good a time as any. Not like I'll be getting any sleep anyway. The last time Daryl invited one of his mates for a "drink," they went on a six-day bender and his security guy called me from a takeaway joint

in Texas saying Daryl had woken up and needed arrange-
ments to get home.

I wish I had left after that, really I should have left way
before that. I don't know why I've hung around these last
two years. I've already made all the contacts I would ever
need, and if I'm honest with myself, I don't even need the
paycheque. If I think about it too much I might end up
admitting that maybe I'm a little afraid to be out there on my
own, or maybe I just like to keep sticking it to daddy dearest
no matter the personal cost.

I scoff and peel away the oversized, ugly, grey blazer. I
hate these suits more than I hate soggy sandwiches, they itch
and are way too big. But fuck it, I don't want to be one of
those girls. I don't want to be another stereotype that relied
on her looks or gave a few blowjobs and made it big.

I wanted to learn, I wanted to hold myself in my own
right. I wanted to meet the right people and do the right
thing, work on my craft and land that record deal that would
snowball my career and put my name on everyone's lips. I
wanted to be the envy of every girl and the wet dream of any
man old enough to jerk off all over himself. But after all this
time, all I've accomplished is making myself invisible.

It was always part of the plan to keep myself hidden in
plain sight. Daryl knew who I was when he offered me the
job, and I think he gets a sick sense of joy when he lashes out
at me. I know he's only angry at *them*—but this was meant to
be a steppingstone, not a beat down.

Everyone sees me as Daryl's girl. *"Love."* Fuck, I hate it
when he calls me that. When he snaps his fingers or stands
there scratching his balls. I shudder to think it's probably
because of the layers of STI's he's picked up over the years.

I sit on my bed, open my laptop and look at tomorrow's
schedule and laugh. As if we'll actually be leaving at nine to
go to the studio. I don't even know why he has me doing
these things. I answer a few emails and read through the

contract the lawyer sent over. Another stadium event scheduled for next year, he will no doubt book out.

My heart leaps when I spot an email from Hunter and settles when I realise it's from his company. It's a standardised, non-personal compliance document and non-disclosure agreements, which should have been done a week ago. The thought of him in that other room makes my stomach roll.

The music thumps through my door like it wants to burst inside and I snap the laptop shut trying to remember the last time I had fun but nothing seems to come up. Not since Uni and that was…. Too long ago. I sigh and think about all those people on the other side of the door. Those famous rockers other people would pay good money to hang out with just sitting a few hundred meters away, laughing and drinking and smoking and kissing and fucking all those half-naked girls. Hunter's face flashes behind my eyes and I snap them open.

I don't want to think about him. About his broad shoulders and muscular arms, about his angled jaw and the small dimple he gets when he smiles. I don't want to think about how he might look now—sweaty and panting, with his neck corded and his blonde hair falling over his green eyes. But I do. I think about him in that room with those women. My thighs clench and my nipples harden, and I suck in a long breath.

I shouldn't wonder, but my hand slinks down on its own, not caring about my brain. My fingers feather over my underwear, feeling the heat and wanting more than just a brief touch. I press them to the fabric, my breath stutters and my door bursts open. The muted music exploding inside as two mostly naked girls and a drunk Dexter Stone fall into my room.

I snatch my hand away, "Get out!" I scream and feel the heat as it floods my cheeks and stings the tip of my ears.

"It's a party baby, come join us," Dexter slurs and winks at me.

"I said get out." I stand and march towards them holding the door and ushering them out.

The girls giggle and turn away, and I hear their laughter as one of them mentions my sad little party for one. The heat burns my face again and I slam my door. Ensuring it's locked, I jump on my bed and bury my face in the pillow wanting to be invisible again.

I wake up feeling like I haven't slept at all. The noise and music from Daryl's drink buddies lasted till well into the early hours of the morning. I shower and dress, pull my hair up into a tight bun and slip my blazer on like it might protect me from Daryl's lashing tongue. I wish he'd stop punishing me for things that aren't my fault. Another fun day of being treated like shit ahead.

I suck in a galvanising breath and walk out of my room. The house is quiet and as I walk through the corridor, I see evidence of the savagery I shielded myself from last night. Discarded clothes and bottles line the corridor, trodden cigarette buds and a looming red stain that's going to cost a shit-tonne to get out of the polished, wooden floor.

I walk by *the* room. The room I know Hunter is still likely to be sleeping in, wrapped around four women. My stomach twists, I shudder and quicken my steps. Downstairs the lounge area looks like a bomb site. Bodies strewn everywhere, slouched and draped over the furniture and the floor. More bottles, more clothing, more stains. Somewhere outside there is a giggle and a splash followed by a deep growl and a shriek. I guess not everyone is done having their fun.

I shake my head and weave my way through the carnage

and into the kitchen where I make myself a cup of coffee and snap open my laptop. I sip on my hot drink and find the number for the cleaning company I used the last time Daryl had one of his "chilled" nights. They are quick, efficient and most importantly discrete. The thought only makes me think of Hunter and that I'd have to run it all by him. Background checks and whatnot.

I run a hand over my face and let it slide to my neck and shoulder where I squeeze the muscles, tension already gripping me.

"Ugh," I look up at the ceiling and let my neck roll from side to side. When I look down, Hunter is standing at the kitchen door with an amused smirk on his face. "What?"

"Nothing." He shrugs and steps deeper into the kitchen where he goes to the coffee machine. He looks fresh like he's had a full night's sleep. Despite wearing yesterday's clothes. His navy-blue t-shirt still looks crisp and his jeans cling to him perfectly. I pry my eyes away from his ass and stare back at my screen, the words turning to blurry black worms. I rub my eyes and take an irritated sip from my coffee. I gulp and for a split-second think that maybe he did just sleep all night, maybe those women didn't interest him. Till he steps a little closer and I see the fading bite mark on his neck.

I huff and he shoots me a look. "What? Didn't you have fun last night?"

"Unlike some people, I don't go sticking my cock in everything that moves."

"Wait? You have a cock?" he tilts his head as if looking for a bulge in my pants.

"Don't be daft." I bristle as he chuckles.

"Hey, it's fine I don't judge."

"I don't have a cock."

"Well, prove it. Otherwise, I'll never be sure"

"Why? You didn't see enough last night?" I hate that I can't tamper the jealousy in my voice.

"No. I didn't see any cocks last night, just a bunch of beautiful women," he throws me a smug smile. "Jealous?"

Arrogant idiot. "Yeah, right."

"Sure? Cause I think I see your cock starting to twitch under your skirt there."

I look down like a complete idiot, and he bursts into full-blown laughter. I'm mortified.

"Asshole." I snap. He keeps laughing, ignoring my comment completely. I suck in a deep breath trying to push some of the embarrassment down. "I'll have to get a cleaning crew in here today."

He wipes his eyes and shakes his head, settling down his laughter, "Just send an email to my office with all the details and we can run the checks on everyone."

"I know. I don't need you telling me how to do my job."

His smile diminishes a little, "I wasn't—"

He starts but I really don't want to hear what he has to say. Irritation stings me like a needle. "They've worked with us before, and they should be fine to come in."

He clears his throat and his relaxed manner stiffens, "We'll see about that."

"There shouldn't be a problem." I cross my hands over my chest.

"There are procedures."

"I've already gone through them."

"Not with me." He sets his coffee down and his face grows tense. I guess he doesn't like to be told how to do his job either.

"Fine." I give him a look and go back to my laptop. A second later his phone pings and he pulls it out, glancing at the screen. "There. I want to schedule them in for two."

His eyes are still down on his phone. "Good luck with that." He smirks at me, "I won't have time to vet them all till then and I still have to get Rob to go through their files."

I inhale through clenched teeth and grab my phone,

dialling his company's number. A deep, male voice answers and introduces himself as Rob. "Hi Rob, this is Emily Shepard, Mr. Dark's assistant."

"What the hell!"

I ignore Hunter as I listen. Rob asks me how he can help; I feel Hunter's eyes bore into the back of my neck. Heat spills into my back and I feel my cheeks burn. I push the words out, "I need a cleaning crew here at two this afternoon. I've emailed you the company portfolio, employee records, and previous security clearance. If you could please liaise with Hunter as soon as possible so that I can book them in, I'd appreciate it."

"Put the phone down." Hunter hisses at me.

Rob chuckles and then clears his throat when he hears Hunter in the background. He sounds amused when he assures me that he will. I thank him and hang up, then turn back to Hunter who is glaring at me. "There, now I've followed your procedures."

Before he has a chance to speak, his phone rings and I hear a deep male voice rumble on the other hand. His green eyes land on me, anger spilling from them. I grab my laptop and escape from the kitchen leaving him to deal with Rob.

Hunter

It's well after one when the household begins to stir and people scrape themselves off the floor and disappear into the daylight like vampires. I spotted Daryl about an hour ago. He came for a coffee and left for a blow job, mumbling something about cleaning the old pipes before a workday. I can relate. Blow jobs make everything better. My cock twitches as it remembers last night, and a smile tries to creep on my face but it's too tired.

I'm fucking falling apart on the inside, exhaustion tugging at all my muscles and pulling on my bleary eyes. This is the kind of day where my coffee needs a coffee, and that's not going to be anywhere near enough to keep me going.

My back keeps searching for a wall to lean against, and I have to work hard to make myself look relaxed instead of asleep on my feet. I just need this day to be over and it hasn't even really begun. The run-in with Emily this morning pissed me off. Who the hell does she think she is pulling that stunt with Rob? My eyes narrow and zero in on her as she marches towards me, Daryl following in her wake. Her eyes down like she's afraid of her own shadow, but she didn't seem afraid this morning. I push the thought away, straighten up and square my shoulders ready to get this day done.

We get into the car and I struggle to keep my eyes open during the drive. We take a secondary route which takes longer and I keep pushing my nails into my palm to keep myself awake.

We slink back into the studio and I find comfort against a wall and under the air con. Daryl looks like shit, drawn and haggard, but as soon as he takes that guitar in his hands all of that falls away.

The man is a fucking magician and it's like drugs and alcohol are his magic potions. If I thought he sounded good yesterday I was delusional.

He pulls out his guitar, worn and scarred by time, and in an instant, he's lost in the old wood and her notes. His body seems possessed, his fingers strum the strings freely creating melodies, and when he sings his voice is velvet and delicious.

The session feels endless like I have fallen in the middle of an ocean and I can't pick a direction, so I just keep treading water. My tiredness makes me hang limp against the wall and my bleary eyes keep finding Emily. She's trying to camouflage herself with the couch—they're the same shade of ash, like maybe they're both burnt out.

She's stretched out, her shoes discarded, her legs crossed over at the ankles. She has long legs and my gaze travels the length of them. They are toned and tanned and sexy and I rip my eyes away convinced that I must be tired.

Daryl screeches through the microphone and demands food. Emily shoots up and slips her feet into her stupid comfortable shoes then comes toward the door. My stomach grumbles and coffee would be a lifesaver. I need to recharge; I feel like my brain is on five percent battery.

She walks by me without a glance, and I run my hand over my stubbled chin. What's her problem? She got her cleaning crew, didn't she? Rob sent the email through and I got a notification that they arrived at five. I roll my eyes at no one and inhale a lungful of cigarette smoke as Daryl walks into the room and lands on the couch. Fucking Daryl.

Twenty minutes later the boys let me know Emily is back and I swing the door open for her, my body craving sustenance. She walks by me like I'm a fucking ghost and hands everyone else their coffees and Korean takeaways which smells fucking delicious and wreaks havoc on my insides. I suddenly long for the cigarette smoke. At least that didn't make me want to eat.

I excuse myself and change over with one of the boys while I go grab something from the employee kitchen. A weak-ass tea and white bread with some jam. I rip through my sandwich and gulp the gooey bread as it breaks down in my mouth. Maybe her cock is taped up too tight. The next few hours feel like a lifetime and when we finally climb back in the car I know I won't be getting enough sleep tonight.

Tom pulls away into the dark streets streaked by flashing lights and colour. The humming of the engine and endless dark road threatens to lull me to sleep.

"Hunter." Daryl's voice tears me from my lethargy.

"Yes sir?"

"Did you like today's session?"

"I did, very much." I'm not just feeding his ego. It's the truth.

He sighs and nods and somehow that sigh carries a harsh, heavy weight that I do not understand.

<hr>

Emily

The house is quiet when we arrive. I know it won't last as Daryl is already on the phone with a "mate," and I've been informed that Dexter Stone will be arriving momentarily. I delight in watching Hunter's face contort in frustration and enjoy it even more when I see the door shut behind him.

The leftover beef Bulgogi is just the right combination of sweet and sour and goes down a treat. I can't help the smile that settles itself on my face every time I think of Hunter's face dropping as I walked right by him with the food earlier. It's definitely making the food taste better.

I was right the first time. He is a meathead with a bad attitude and attempting to be nice was a mistake I will not be repeating again. Condescending idiot. Walking around the house uninvited, in his tight jeans and bite marks all over his neck looking fresh as a fucking daisy, with his stupid sexy forearm muscles and refusing to give me my cleaning crew.

Hunter Evans is a typical bouncer, with his mind only on looking pretty and sleeping with random tarts.

8

—————

Hunter

I pull up to the house, to find only one car in the driveway —Daryl's. As I make my way inside, the place looks like it did the first day we arrived, immaculate. I smell coffee and bacon. The aroma filters through me and seeps into every pore. I walk through the pristine house towards the kitchen where I find Emily and freeze.

She's leaning over the counter, a cup of hot coffee in one hand and a plate of crispy bacon in the other. One of the thin straps of the tiny white singlet she's wearing, falls over a naked shoulder. The singlet shows off her curvy waist and a sliver of skin. I swallow hard as my graze tracks downwards. A silk black thong clings to her perfectly round ass and shows off her long, bare legs.

"I made this for you, just the way you like it." She purrs and sucks on her lower lip.

My eyes snap open and it takes me a few seconds to realise I'm in my bed...alone.

"What the fuck was that?" I rub the sleep from my eyes just to have an image of Emily in that singlet floating in the darkness. My body feels hard and tight.

My alarm goes off and I punch it off, maybe a little harder than I intended. I roll out of bed, my throbbing cock hard and painful as I make my way to the shower. Two problems I can solve in one place.

I stand under the hot stream and let the water pelt my skin and wash away my annoyance.

It's been an exhausting week and never have I wanted a job to end as much as this one. My body hurts. I'm tired of Daryl's impromptu drinking sessions that go on for hours or days and leave me drained and irritable. I can't pretend I don't enjoy the occasional girl he throws my way and the use of his lavish spare room, but I'm wrecked.

Then there's Emily, I can't figure her out, and now I can't get that image of her out of my head.

Fuck it, the sooner this day starts the sooner it finishes.

I turn off the water and towel off wondering what bull-shit I'll have thrown at me today.

***

An eerie feeling of DeJaVu ripples through me as I pull up to the house just before eight. I'm instantly annoyed and relieved to see a bunch of cars in the drive-way. Daryl and his fucking parties. I guess I should be used to it by now, but his nonchalant attitude grates me the wrong way. My phone has a hundred different notifications that accumulated overnight, emails about people coming and going. I don't bother going through them, if anything major happened someone would have come knocking on my door.

I draw in a steeling breath preparing myself for another day of waiting and getting fucked around. This is bullshit.

Wolf should be doing this, not me—another week till that overgrown asshat is back.

I step into the disaster zone, which is the house, just as two tanned, giggling brunettes in bikinis push by me. I smile at them and they look me up and down before disappearing down the driveway and into a waiting taxi outside the main gate. I hope they'll be back later.

I step into the kitchen and stall for a second as I spot Emily. She's in another one of her boring suits, perched on her stool, a coffee cup in her hand, and her eyes glued to her screen. No bacon in sight. I shake my head, dislodging remnants of my dream and step across the threshold.

Her head turns and she smiles at me. That's suspicious.

"Good morning." She chirps.

"Good morning?" I have to say that I'm a little confused by her warmth after a week of hard glares and cold shoulder tactics.

She swivels her body around and her crossed legs straighten in front of her, I clear my throat and find her eyes.

"So," she starts and I know my day is about to get ruined, "Daryl would like to change the schedule for tonight - just a little dinner and maybe a show."

"No," I state bluntly, and her smile fades a little. I've noticed I have that effect on her.

"Why?" she replies.

Why? For a hundred different fucking reasons. Because she wants to play games because she wants to shove the fact I'm the hired help in my face because she haunts me in my dreams and because there is no fucking bacon. Suddenly getting under her skin feels like the most important task of my day. I settle on, "It's not enough notice, I don't have the details—"

"I emailed everything to you an hour ago."

I grind my teeth. "I haven't had time to go through my emails yet."

"Well, maybe you should start work a little earlier."

My fists ball at my sides, "I need to sleep sometimes."

"You'd sleep more if you stopped shagging every girl here and did your job properly." At that, I tear the distance between us in two strides and loom over her, backing her up against the wall with my hands caging her there. My chest rises and falls with my sharp intake of breath.

"What I do outside of my work hours is none of your business, I do my job just fine," I grit out through a clenched jaw. "And the answer to your request is still no."

She hits my chest with her fists and tries to push me away. I laugh. When she lifts her hands a second time, I think she might slap me. On instinct I grab her wrists and pin them over her head, forcing her body up, pulling at her shoulders so that she has to stand on her tiptoes.

Her eyes round and widen as she glares up at me and she bites on her lower lip—heat simmers between us.

I stare into her eyes, and for the first time, I notice how their centre is like deep caramel that spreads out into honey hues and breaks against the outer edge of dark roasted coffee beans. She hides so much behind those beautiful eyes.

I'm suddenly very aware of her body against mine, her hot breath fanning my chest, her heated eyes glaring into mine. Without thinking, my hand slithers down and beneath her shirt where my finger brushes her delicate skin just below the belly button. She gasps at the intrusion, and I tear my hand away. *What the fuck am I doing?* She blinks and all the warmth in her eyes disappears.

"Okay," she breathes out and pulls at her hands. I release her wrists and she pushes my chest forcefully; I don't move but smirk at her effort. She huffs out an irritated sound before she ducks under my arm and storms out of the kitchen.

What the fuck was that?

I let out a sharp breath allowing my heart rate to settle. It seems like she's the only woman that keeps wanting to get away from me. Luckily, I don't care. What I do care about is my morning coffee and getting this day over and done with. I pour myself a cup, pull out my phone and scroll through my emails, finding the one from Emily.

It's a reservation for 9 pm to one of London's best and most exclusive restaurants. The email is meticulous. She's included every detail I need to get this done. She makes it easy, easier than most other people I've had to work with. I haven't had a client's P.A this efficient since Mr. Legend. I flick it over to Rob as a top priority, and I'm about to call him when Daryl storms into the kitchen with Emily like a shadow hanging behind him. He looks like he's just rolled out of his bed, dishevelled and pissed.

"Good morning, Sir."

"Yeah, it's not. I want to go eat tonight, I have an important meeting. I hear that's an unreasonable request, and you can't get it fucking done?"

I shot Emily a hard look, did she just grass on me to her boss? I tuck my shaking hands behind my back and steady my breath before I answer.

"No sir, there appears to have been a miscommunication. I've already passed the information on to my local team who will start canvassing the place and get what needs to be done, to ensure you can enjoy your night out safely."

I can feel Emily's eyes burning into me, but I ignore her. This will not be the victory she thought she was going to have.

"Right," Daryl spins back, "why the fuck did you wake me then, love? I'll deal with you later." He throws at her before storming off.

We stand facing one another for a minute, her eyes burning with hatred while I pull out my best 'fuck you' smirk. Something about the way she is looking at me tugs at my body, it remembers the dream much too vividly. I wonder if I can fuck all that anger out of her. The thought makes my dick come to life and it pushes uncomfortably against my jeans.

Somewhere in the house a door slams. The noise is enough to pull us out of the moment, and Emily turns away and disappears into the house.

Fuck this job.

Daryl isn't ready on time and I can't say that I'm surprised. I stand outside with Tom leaning against the car. He's talking about his daughter's birthday party. His face lights up when he talks about his family. It's sweet. He's renting a pony for her and her friends and for a moment I think about all of Red's birthday parties. Me and her huddled on the couch eating a cupcake and watching an action movie till late. Until her sixteenth birthday, I couldn't give her more. She'd never asked for more before - and never after.

The door swings open and Daryl steps outside. His long hair is brushed haphazardly and he's wearing his trademark jeans and a worn metal T-shirt, he gives zero fucks that he's about to walk into an establishment that charges £1000 just to breathe the air. But something else catches my eye. I don't recognise her at first and when I do something yanks at the inside of my stomach and I can't help but stare.

Her hair is longer than I thought and it's the first time she's worn it down since I've seen her. It's brown with natural highlights and flows well beyond her shoulders in beautiful waves. Her face is naturally made up and highlights her eyes and full lips. Her lipstick glints in the lights and she licks her lips like she's nervous. My whole body tightens at the slight action. She's wearing a black shirt that falls over a black mini skirt and long black boots that show just enough of her thigh to have my imagination trying to fill in gaps it shouldn't.

A slew of images smash through me, a naked Emily bent over and all the sounds I can force out of her pouty little lips. I tear my gaze away from her and wait for them to get into the car before I can adjust, then take my seat upfront with Tom.

We get to the restaurant forty minutes late and we get ushered inside as if we're royalty and time doesn't apply to us. Daryl gets seated at a table where a tall leathery man awaits. He looks like a snake, all sharp angles and narrow eyes. Something about him makes all the hair on my body stand to attention and my muscles clump together ready to pounce. Emily and I get ushered to a secondary table.

"Shouldn't you be sitting with your boss?" I turn to her as she sits down and crosses her long legs over.

She shakes her head, "No thanks. It's not my kind of meeting."

I have no idea what that means and I don't really care. I'm vaguely aware of the fact that my body keeps wanting to get closer to hers. I ignore the feeling and wave away the hovering waiter before I grab the water jug from his hand and pour us both a glass of water, then turn my attention back to Daryl. He's leaning back without a care in the world, a smile plastered across his face as his companion speaks.

We sit in silence—for some it might be uncomfortable, but it suits me just fine. Not having to engage in small talk while I watch a client, works for me. Not to mention, it's likely anything she says is going to piss me off. Most other women like to talk your ear off and discuss mundane, uninteresting subjects. Emily doesn't seem to want to tell me anything. I ignore her, though every now and then I can't help but steal a glance at her.

She's flicked her long hair over her shoulders and it accentuates her long neck. For a second I find myself wondering what it might feel like to kiss it. Women are like ice cream, each with their own unique flavour and I bet she would taste so fucking sweet. I try to shake the thought away but she looks fucking delectable. I shift in my seat as I take in her features and remind myself that the last thing I need is some smitten colleague that will cling on to me till my last day of work. Fraternising with the other staff is a no-no. I've learned my lesson plenty of times with sulking bar managers and waitresses. I smirk. After all, I'm a glutton for punishment and they were gluttons for my dick. I shrug all the thoughts away and divert my attention back to Daryl.

This place offers a set menu of twelve dishes. They come accompanied by the perfect wine. We had a look at the menus before we left the house and she already knows exactly what we are going to be served. She's not the kind of person that leaves things to chance, so I have no idea why she needs to read over it again. I watch her study the menu and her lips pout ever so slightly as if she's imagining what the food might taste like. I find myself wondering what she might taste like. I clear my throat and drink my water, washing the thought away and stare at Daryl. He's on his second beer and we've been here less than fifteen minutes.

They bring out the first dish and Emily can't hide behind the menu anymore. Instead, she stared animatedly into her plate as if it's the most riveting thing she's ever seen. I take a bite of the entrée. It's delicious. This is one of those places where the food looks better than you but only takes up an 1/8th of the plate. After a few bites, you're done but the flavour is so intense, it's like you can only handle one mouthful at a time.

They clear the plates from our first dishes. Daryl seems relaxed. No one seems to be paying him any attention apart from his dinner guest.

"Were you a soldier?" I startle at the sound of her voice and my gaze flickers over to her.

"No, why?"

She shrugs, "The way you move maybe, it's a little…rigid."

"Rigid?" I ask in a stiff voice and immediately regret it.

She shrugs.

"I'm not rigid. I have good posture." I groan inwardly. Did I really just say that?

A ghost of a smile touches her lips and she wipes it away with a swipe of her tongue. My cock twitches and I don't know if I'm annoyed or turned on. "If you say so."

Irritation prickles my skin, and I run my hand on my thighs trying to dispel some of it. I still have to sit here with her for the next three hours.

"If not the military, then how did you get into this line of work?"

I try not to sigh, maybe she is just like the rest of them after all. "My partner and I have a knack for this. Guess in some way we've always been protecting people."

She studies my face and her eyes widen just a fraction, leaning in, her eyes study my face full of questions she's not asking.

For some reason, I start talking. "My parents abandoned my sister and I when we were very young. My grandmother came to look after us but got sick, so it kind of fell on me to look after her. I guess protecting people was just second nature after that."

"That must have been hard."

"I did what I needed to do." I shrug off her comment.

"Not everyone would." She counters and I know she's right.

"It didn't feel like a chore if that's what you mean. Sure, there were lots of other things I wanted to do. But Red was the easy decision every time. She's my sister—my family. It wasn't even a choice."

She nods taking in my words and her eyes still search my face like she's trying to find something that's not there.

"Doing what you know you're supposed to do regardless of what you want, that takes conviction."

Conviction? "Like I said, it wasn't a choice."

Our second course arrives interrupting our conversation, I polish it off in two mouthfuls. Emily takes her time studying the artwork on her plate. It's a waste of time, in about three seconds it will all be gone, but still, she takes it all in, the carefully constructed tiny mountain on her plate. She scoops a minute portion onto her fork and it vanishes between her plump lips. Her eyes shut and I think I hear her purr a little. My stomach clenches at how irritatingly fucking sexy that is, I shuffle in my seat, tear my eyes away and stare at her boss who instantly cools my insides.

"So," she starts and I groan inwardly not wanting to give her more than I already let slip, "how long have you and your partner been together?"

"Since we were at school together."

"So, first love?"

"Love? Wait, what? No, we're not that kind of partners."

"It's ok, I don't judge."

"He's my best friend."

"It's important to build your relationship on friendship, makes the relationship more than just superficial."

"Emily." I warn her, but she smirks at me and reaches for her wine.

I could ask her about her life or her family, and try to get to know her, but after that, I think it's pointless, she's clearly only interested in getting under my skin, and like an idiot, I walked right into it. In four and a half weeks she'll be the annoying PA that gave me shit and I can move on. So I keep glaring at Daryl who is perfectly safe in his seat and avoid any further conversation.

We're on the seventh course and I notice Emily's eyes start to glaze over slightly, the volume of alcohol served with each meal far greater than the foods we've actually been ingesting. She's clearly a lightweight. She hasn't been as chatty as I thought she was going to be and I'm grateful. She keeps surprising me. It's rare and also a little frustrating.

Most people are predictable; they have behaviours that repeat, patterns, habits, regimented conversations they have with people they meet and others they avoid altogether. Yet she's been a little bit of everything. Hot, cold, interested, disinterested, funny, serious. She's giving me whiplash.

"I need the little girl's room," she announces a little more to the room than to me. A few heads turn and she giggles then stands up. A little unsteady on her feet.

"Maybe I should help you," I say and stand up.

"I've been going to the toilet all by myself for the last twenty-five years, I think I can manage."

"I'm sure you can," I say but I don't sit down. I flash another look at Daryl. Still fine.

I escort Emily to the bathroom, a narrow dim corridor tucked in at the back of the restaurant. It feels like a back alley in a posh neighbourhood. It's clean but you know dodgy shit still happens here. I lean against the wall and wait for her, questioning why I'm out here when I should be keeping an eye on my client, the one I'm actually being paid to watch.

I find myself not really wanting to answer my own question, so I push the thought away just as she comes sauntering out of the bathroom. She sees me and her face stretches into a sweet smile. I frown. I think I need to get her home. She walks toward me, and her shoe gets caught on the carpet. I could let her fall, punish her for trying to make me look like a fool this morning, but I don't. Instead, I rush in and, with a sweep of my arm, grab her and pull her into me.

Our bodies are flush, and my heart trips as her eyes land on mine. They're wide and round and the caramel swirls inside them as they slowly lower to my mouth. She drags her teeth over her lower lip and her eyes snap back to mine. I have a sudden craving for ice cream. An unfamiliar wave of desire—like lightning—strikes my insides and charges me with wild electricity that needs an outlet. I grab her chin and before I know what I'm doing I kiss her, hard.

I hate the way I love how she tastes. She's so fucking sweet, like honey and caramel. Her hands thread around my neck then rake into my hair as she opens up for me and allows me to deepen our kiss. She kisses me back, delicate and hungry all at the same time, and I feel the need to consume her—all of her. I want more. So much more, which is why I break our kiss and step away. We can't do this. I can't do this. Not with her.

I hold her an arm's length and wipe my mouth with the back of my hand. "What the hell are you doing?"

For a second she looks confused. "What?"

"Why the hell are you kissing me?"

She blinks a few times as if she doesn't understand what I said, before her brow creases "You kissed me." She spits back, her voice full of venom and confusion.

"I don't fraternise with employees; whatever you think this is, it's not. You've obviously had too much to drink." The words taste like shit in my mouth as I say them, but I know it's the right thing to do.

Her face turns a shade of pink and melts from happiness to confusion to embarrassment to anger. It's like watching an ice sculpture melt under a blow torch. She shakes her head and says nothing else as she storms out of the dim corridor.

I run my hands over my face. "Fuck." I can be something to other people, but not her. She's the hired help, like me, and we're both disposable. I have a reputation to keep, a business to run—this can't happen.

When I come out of the corridor and towards our table, I find it empty. I shoot a look towards Daryl's table. Empty.

Fuck

Where the hell is he? I scan the room and see him

standing at another table signing an autograph for some girl. She rolls her tongue over her lips and he bends over to whisper in her ear. She giggles, and I roll my eyes.

I find Emily by the coat check, heading towards the door. I march over and grab her elbow, "What do you think you're doing?"

"Leaving," She hisses at me and tries to pry her elbow out. When I release her, she stumbles from the shifting balance and I catch her for a second time, pulling her into me and getting a whiff of her shampoo.

I grit my teeth as she swings at my chest, "Let me go."

Holding onto her, I lead her outside and find Tom waiting by the car. I instruct him to take her back to the house and then return for me and Daryl. He nods and I slide Emily into the back seat. Her long legs are smooth, and soft and I have a sudden need to run my hands all over them. But she slaps me away before the thought can take hold.

"I don't need any help," she grinds out through a gritted jaw and shuffles to the other end of the car.

I close the car door and Tom takes off. When I get back inside, Daryl and the woman are missing.

I scan the restaurant and when I can't find him I make my way to the bathrooms. Inside, I hear all the confirmation I need that I've found my client. I lean against the door and stop anyone who tries to get inside, earning me dirty looks and a visit from the manager.

I shrug him off and keep the toilet door closed. When they emerge, the woman's hair is a mess and she is wiping at her mouth. Daryl is smiling like he's just won some kind of blow job lottery, and all my nerves are crackling with agitation under my skin.

When she tries to hang onto him, I secure Daryl, placing myself between the two of them before I escort him outside and to the car. He tries to protest, but I don't give a fuck. I'm done with tonight and all I can think about is caramel ice cream.

Emily

My head feels fuzzy. I groan and turn onto my back, feeling a wet patch on my cheek. I swipe away the drool and open a single eye, reaching for my phone. 9.13 a.m. *Shit.* I bolt up. I overslept. I never oversleep. But then I take another look at the date. It's Saturday.

I let the phone drop from my hand and stretch my arms over my head, arching my back. I close my eyes and think about all the work I still have to do. Daryl's upcoming tour 'Drowning in Darkness' has me drowning in contracts for venues, insurance, merchandise and security details.

Fucking security. I flashback to last night. Hunter's lips on mine, the way he tasted and felt against me. *'What the hell are you doing?'* The question punches me in the gut just as it did last night.

But I know he wanted it too. Didn't he?

He kissed *me!*

Or maybe I imagined it all? The way his eyes dipped to my lips and how his hands cupped my chin, and how he leaned in closing the distance till our lips collided. I shake the thought away. He's right. Of course, we shouldn't have kissed. We work together and that shit never ends well. I have a plan. I have a path and he's just a pretty boy that will finish this job and move on elsewhere with more half-naked women to keep him occupied.

Except that he isn't really. Not when you talk to him. Not when he lets you glimpse a little bit of what goes on inside his head. It's almost like behind his robotic stance, an actual human exists. He mentioned that he's an orphan, that he has a sister. He's had battles and demons, and he's come from nothing to build a hugely successful company. That takes a lot of tenacity, determination and hard work.

Whereas I came from privilege. A perfect bird in a gilded prison, a product of love and hate, of betrayal and pain. I have a bursting bank account full of guilt money. I've never worked out if he was trying to buy my love or my forgiveness. Either way, my father keeps offering to usher me into his world, to open all the doors, and shove me through them. Yet, like Hunter, I want to battle, to fight, I want to make it on my own. He'll only ever see me as a poor little rich girl.

I sigh. After this tour, I'll start recording. I've already booked a studio, and I promise myself for the hundredth time that I won't reschedule this time around.

Fuck, I can't wait.

I head into the shower and get ready for the day, washing away last night's embarrassment. We're both professionals, it's fine. It will all be over in just four more weeks. All I have to do is not think about it or him—or his soft lips or his strong hands or any other stupid part of him. *How hard can that be?*

I need a day away from everyone. Hunter will be lurking somewhere waiting for Daryl, but that's his problem. I can take the day off. Enjoy this house a little while everyone is still asleep.

I slip on my white bikini and pull my hair up in a messy bun. It is my day off after all, I don't need a suit or makeup. I just want to get out of this heat and cool down my insides, which keep flooding with warmth every time I think about Hunter Evans and the way his body made mine come alive.

I open my door just a fraction and peak down the corridor. It's quiet. The way I like it. I don't want to be confused for one of "their girls." I walk by the room. *That* room and my stomach flutters then knits at the thought of him with those girls. *Why can't I let that go?*

I hold the towel around my waist and go to the kitchen to grab a bottle of water.

I halt when I get to the doorway and stumble over my feet. He's there looking fresh and perfect as always. *Asshole.* Maybe if I ignore him, he'll just keep pretending like I don't exist and we can get this job over and done with. He's sitting on *my* stool. Leaning against the counter where I work, his long legs crossed over casually at the ankles.

I recover and make my way to the fridge, feeling the weight of his stare while I open it and reach for a bottle of water.

"Grab me a bottle while you're there?"

I glare at him, but his focus has shifted to the phone in his hands. I hold the fridge door open, the cool air soothing my heated skin. "Get it yourself, I don't work for you."

"You don't have to work for me to grab me a bottle of water." He doesn't look up and his fingers type something on his phone.

"Well, have you considered saying please?"

He looks up for half a second and a long, lowly smirk stretches across his stupid, beautiful face, "Will you *please* grab me a bottle of water while you're at the fridge?" His tone is condescending, and I consider a few places I could shove that bottle for him.

Still, like I'm on autopilot, I grab a second bottle and walk towards him before handing it over. His big hand wraps around it and his long fingers brush over mine before I have a chance to pull my hand away. I hate how the feel of his hand over mine makes all the muscles in my body tense up.

I take a step back and watch him uncap the bottle and take a swig. It's such a simple gesture, and yet, my eyes are glued to the way the muscles in his neck cord. My fingers itch to glide along them. He recaps the bottle and his lips tip in a smile as he catches me staring.

"You're too trusting, I could have poisoned you."

"Nah." His eyes are back on his phone, and I'm back to being invisible.

"You're so sure of yourself."

He shrugs, "Nah, you're just too predictable."

Fury vibrates through me, his dismissal of me. He doesn't know the first thing about me. "What the hell are you doing here anyway? Where is Daryl?" I snap at him

"Probably still in bed."

"Then why the hell are you here?"

"Cause I can be." His smugness riles me and slithers under my skin. *We'll see about that.*

Ugh. I don't know what else to say. I can deal with him later—after my heartbeat settles down and my body temperature returns to normal. I hate that all I can think about now are his lips and that he makes me feel awkward and uncoordinated, like all my thoughts get clumped together and sense leaks out of my ears into the ether.

He stands as I leave the kitchen and his heavy footsteps echo behind me. I don't dare turn around. Daryl pops up from nowhere and stops me in my tracks. Hunter's movements have also stopped, but I feel his body, it's too close to mine.

"Good morning, love. I'm inspired."

I glare at him already irked by Hunter. Why are all the men in my life assholes? I picture my father's smug face, knowing what he would say. I brush the thought away even more annoyed.

He runs his hand through his long hair a few times as if considering something then his face tilts a little. "Can you be ready in ten minutes?"

I grit my teeth, my fists tightening around the water bottle. "It's my day off."

"Not anymore, love." He winks at me, "Ten minutes, yeah?"

I inhale an agitated breath that does nothing to calm me down, "Of course."

"Chop, chop, love." He claps twice as I storm off to my room and hear their deep voices discussing the plan.

I peel away my bikini and discard it on the bed. It lays there limply. Anger floods through me. *'Chop, chop.'* I want to scream. Instead, I grab one of my suits and throw it on. I don't bother fixing my hair and I take a minute to put on minimal makeup.

I inhale a few long breaths before I go back downstairs, where Hunter stands next to Daryl.

"Ah, good girl," Daryl says and I want to punch him. Or better still, I want Hunter to. I bet he could knock a few teeth out. I climb downstairs pretending I didn't hear him and follow them to the car where Tom has the engine running and the air con on.

We slip inside the car and Tom pulls away. I plaster my face to the window, wondering what I keep waiting for.

Hunter

Tom pulls away from the driveway and we head out to the studio. I'm not sure what got the guy out of bed before midday, but fuck, I'm not complaining. I might actually be able to rest this afternoon. But still, I can't shake my annoyance. Not only at the way Daryl keeps talking to Emily, but the fact that he got her to take that fucking bikini off and put more clothes on. I was enjoying the view. It was rather… unexpected. All her beautiful curves were on display and that outline rose tattoo on her lower back, it was like unravelling a secret. I find myself wanting to know what other secrets she's hiding.

I'm lost in thought when we pull up to the studio. Daryl stomps inside then stands at the door. "Private session today kids, you wait here."

He slams the door in my face. It's not unusual for these people to treat me like shit but I hate that he's dragged Emily here just to lock her outside with me.

"I can have Tom drive you back to the house," I offer my olive branch.

Her eyes snap up to me for a second before her face softens, the fight leaking out before it can begin, "It's fine." She shakes her head and leans against the wall. "I know he seems —" she swirls a hand in the air as if summoning a word from nothing "—unhinged. But he always has a plan. If he wanted me here, there's a reason."

"If you say so." I shrug and take in her features, suddenly not minding the company.

We stand in silence for a while, muted sounds leak from beneath the door. She grabs her phone; it snags on her pocket and drops from her hand. We both go for it at the same time, but I get there a second faster than she does. My eyes fall on the unlocked screen.

"Can I have my phone please?" She's holding her hand out to me while I invade her privacy.

I read the text knowing I shouldn't, "Why do you need this?"

"That's none of your business. Can I have my phone please?" She takes a swipe at me, but I just raise my hand. I'm significantly taller and stronger than she is. She won't be getting her phone back until I decide to give it to her.

"Original song lyrics and composition by Ash Rogers?" I look down at her face, "The lead singer of 'The Broken'?"

She glares at me.

My eyes snap back to the phone, the live auction closes in ten minutes. "The bids are still coming in."

"Give me my phone!"

"Tell me what you're doing." I know it's none of my business, she's right. I really I shouldn't care, but I'm intrigued.

"It's for Daryl," she says and her eyes drop to the floor.

"Liar." Her eyes jerk back to mine and burn into me. "Tick-tock." I shake the phone a little, and she exhales a sharp breath.

"Fine, I collect them."

"Collect what?"

"Song lyrics and compositions."

"Why?"

"Inspiration maybe?"

"Maybe?"

She shrugs, "It motivates me."

"To do what? They're just pieces of paper with other people's words and music."

Her eyes flicker back to the phone before they meet mine again, "Books are also full of other people's words and yet people collect them. We dive into their pages and search for lines of meaning through the concepts, dreams and discord of other people's minds. We travel to the past and the future and collect thoughts, because every now and then one resonates. Like looking in a mirror, we recognise those feelings inside ourselves."

"And these lyrics?"

"They resonate with me."

I look at the title and frown, "*This* resonates with you?"

Her chin tips and her eyes fall away, "It resonates with a lot of people. It's the reason it's one of their biggest hits."

"It's not that great." I think about the lyrics, *I always grow attached to things that aren't forever.* "Not exactly profound."

"That's because you don't get attached to the things you collect."

I scoff, "I don't collect anything."

"Sure you do, everyone collects."

"Yeah? What do I collect?"

"Women, STI's, and angry encounters."

I scoff, "I don't collect women, they try to collect me. I'm more of a connoisseur, I like to sample." My gaze automatically runs along her body. "Isn't it better to spend my time with women than with useless pieces of paper? And FYI, I've never had an STI."

Her mouth twists a little and she takes a tiny step back as if I'd pushed her. She doesn't even notice it. "If you say so. Can I have my phone back now?"

I glance at the screen, we still have time, and I have more questions. Questions she's more likely to answer if I have this hold over her. Is it fair? Probably not, but who said life has to be? "Soon." She sighs and her mouth stretches into a thin line. I ignore her. "Why do you stay?"

"With Daryl?"

I nod.

"The money is good." Her eyes dart around the corridor again.

"He treats you like shit."

"It's fine."

"It's not," I raise my voice a little too much, and her eyes collide with mine for a second before they fall away.

"It's fine. Why do you care anyway?"

"Because it's bullshit, he shouldn't be treating you like that."

She shrugs.

"Why do you stay?"

She stays silent.

"Tick-tock, Emily." I shake the phone at her. She grimaces and glares at me. I'm prying, but I want to know why she puts up with his shit. She is clearly intelligent and sweet and has a lot to offer. So why him?

"It's complicated."

I frown at her secrecy, what is she hiding? "Why?"

"It just is." Pink floods her cheeks and she looks around, refusing to meet my eyes. "Can I get my phone back?"

I glance at it, two minutes. I check the bid as it climbs, already well past the fifteen thousand dollar mark.

"Tell me!"

Her eyes flash to the phone, desperation etched on her features. "Not that it's any of your business, but I needed a way in, and this was an easy door to walk through."

"A way into what?"

She grinds her teeth. "I want to sing," she spits it out, "now give me my phone." She wines as the screen flashes red.

"You? Sing?" I'm surprised, but it comes out condescending.

"Yes," she hisses, "phone!" She puts her hand out, her eyes widening as the screen keeps flashing red.

I can't help but scoff under my breath.

"Are you laughing at me?"

"You? Stand in front of people and perform? You can't even walk around in a bikini without hiding behind a towel like it's going to save your life."

"I don't need to show off my body to be good at singing," she snaps at me.

"No, but it helps." I wink at her—clearly a mistake.

I shake my head and that's when she takes me by surprise, her elbow flies into my stomach and she jumps up and snatches the phone from me. I laugh at her antics, but she ignores me, tapping on her phone frantically as the numbers count down. Maybe mousy Emily isn't as shy as she makes herself out to be.

She holds her breath and stares at the screen, her knuckles bleached white, her eyes bulging. We wait in silence before she breaks it with a yelp and a little dance. She hugs the phone to her chest and relief floods her face, followed by a stunning, happy smile. I can't help but smile too.

"I got it. I got it." She squeals as if she's totally forgotten that I held her phone hostage just a few seconds ago. How the fuck could she afford that on her salary? I set the thought aside and watch her. She's radiating. I think it's the first time I've seen Emily happy. Somehow that smile transforms her, and she just went from pretty to beautiful. She's beautiful when she's happy, and my body remembers that kiss and how her lips felt against mine, and how I could make her happy in other ways.

"Love!" Daryl's voice breaks through my thoughts and the smile that made her face beam falls away in an instant. "I need you in here."

"Coming," she calls out and tucks away her phone, her eyes meeting mine as if she's just remembered I was there. She opens her mouth as if she's about to say something then changes her mind before grabbing the door handle and slipping into the studio, shutting me alone with my thoughts.

Emily

I don't have time to dwell on all my feelings. My anger is now doused by happiness, by confusion and irritation. I'll have to sort through them all later. As of right now, I have to deal with Daryl. I tune back into what he's saying.

"—a backup singer that can get here now?"

"It's eleven on a Saturday morning in London Daryl, you'll have more luck finding a black cat in a coal cellar."

"But it's London, love. It's full of wannabes."

"And do you have their numbers? Do you have time to

audition?" I purse my lips, "I guess I can call a few agencies, see what they send over."

He runs a hand through his hair as I pull out my phone. "Hang on love, you're a singer ain't you?"

"I—"

"Great, get in there then, lemme run you through the lyrics."

"Daryl..."

"Here are the lyrics I want you to sing." He shoves a crumpled piece of paper into my hands with frantically scribbled words running across the page.

I read over them as he leads me into the studio.

"Fantastic. Come on, love, let's get to work. This will be fantastic." For the first time, he looks at me like he sees me and not *her*. His smile is genuine and real and my heart leaps a little.

The next three hours are exhausting and thrilling in equal measure. I've been dreaming of being on this side of the glass booth—not as Daryl's backup singer, but for myself. Still, belting out his chorus and hearing it played back to me exhilarates me in ways that I can't fathom. It feels like breaking the surface and drawing a lungful of air after staying under for too long.

As we head back to the car, Hunter gives me a long look before shuffling his massive frame into the front seat. I forgot about him for a few hours and now that we share the same space, the delight I've been feeling all afternoon is threatened by his presence.

I stare out the window and try to forget him and his prying and his arrogance. He laughed at me. *Whatever.*

"You did great, love," Daryl pulls me from my reverie, "You have a great set of pipes on you. Your dad will be proud."

Hunter shuffles in his seat, his head turns slightly towards us.

"Thanks." I bite the inside of my cheek, hoping the other two people in the car don't know what he means.

"Sure I can't talk you into being a backup for me? You can join me on tour."

I shake my head, "If I went on tour with you, who would get all your contracts signed and venues booked?"

He laughs a little and pats my leg. I resist the urge to remove his hand forcefully and elbow his jaw. "You can taste what it's like. You can be set on fire. There's nothing like being on stage with people chanting your name, worshipping you." He shakes his head, "And nothing ignites you as hot as your first performance. It's like falling in love for the first time, and you'll never forget it."

There's something melancholy in his voice as he speaks. "I'd rather my first time be under my own terms."

He locks eyes with me and nods, "As it should be. I'll find someone. Book some auditions for next week won't you?"

"Sure," I say, "Will you be needing anything else from me this afternoon?"

"Nah, Love, you've worked hard enough, take the rest of the day. Go out, relax." He winks at me and I turn away.

Tom pulls up to the house and I get out of the car slamming the door behind me and rushing inside. A part of me wants to show them both, to prove them wrong, to be the person I know I can be.

The house is quiet, the guests that crashed over have vacated, and the cleaning crew have somehow managed to reorganise this place. Again. I make a mental note to send them all gifts when we leave this place. I get to my room and throw off my suit, grabbing my bikini and sliding it back on. The day has been so hot, my body is on fire. A dip in the pool will help cool me down.

I grab my towel, throwing it over my shoulder this time. I don't need to hide behind it, I don't want to. I go past the kitchen and grab my bottle of water before I head outside and set my towel down on one of the deck chairs.

The cold water engulfs me and for a split second, it feels as if my heart has seized. I didn't expect it to be so cold. I suck in a long breath and push off the wall, sinking deeper until I'm inches off the bottom. I swim, pushing my body through the water, propelling myself forward. In this muted world my clumped thoughts fall to pieces and rearrange themselves. The stillness fills me with tranquillity, nothing can touch me down here.

I feel the agitation of the last few days peel off my skin, dissolve into nothingness, till all that remains is my determination. I flip over and push off the opposite wall. My heart hammers against my ribs, my lungs burning, needing oxygen, but I want to keep fighting. I want to stay in control, I want to earn that first breath. Breaking the surface should feel rewarding, like I've earned it, not been spoon-fed. Anger ripples inside me as I think of Hunter's laughter and I push the thought away into the blue, drowning it. Every cell in my body screams for oxygen, I push up and break the surface, gulping at the hot summer air. It floods my body like relief and I know that this is how I want to feel when I first get on stage. Like I'm alive.

I do a few more laps. On my last turn, I spot Hunter standing by the window, talking to Daryl and watching me with rapt attention. His gaze makes me feel like a small boat on a very big, turbulent ocean. Feeling the weight of his gaze is like sitting and waiting for a forceful tsunami to come and tip me over. He confuses me. One moment he's volatile and hostile and makes me want to rip his head off, the next he's glaring at Daryl for treating me like shit, opening up about his past and kissing me in corridors, leaving me raw and disarmed.

I let out a lungful of air, setting a stream of bubbles bursting along my face before I float face down with my thoughts on the surface of the water, blocking both of them from my mind.

<hr>

Hunter

Daryl has a 'chat.' A whole lot of nothing words he throws my way. With all his many friends and parties the guy seems really lonely. I hope he doesn't plan on making that problem mine. I'm happy to watch his back, but I'm not here to be his friend or confidant. I have enough of those. Wolf is getting back mid next week and it can't come early enough. Red might also give me the time of day, she still hasn't forgiven me for the time she says I stole from them. She'll come around, eventually; she always does.

I rub my eyes and glance at the pool. My heart seizes. Emily is floating face down in the water, her body bobbing in the rippling blue. A million questions thunder inside me as I leap away from Daryl and sprint towards the patio. Where the fuck is everyone else? Why is no one watching? How long has she been face down? Fuck.

The cold water rips my breath away and my clothes stick to my body making it harder to move. I'm on her in a second and I tear her from the water spinning her face up.

I don't expect resistance.

She's clawing at me and her body tightens in my grasp, she sucks in a breath, her face a mask of confusion and surprise.

"What the hell are you doing?" she screams at me as the realisation dawns and my blood floods with heat.

"I thought you were... I was..." but she's pulling herself out of my grasp and not listening.

"I don't need your help," she snaps at me and starts to swim away, but I realise that I don't want to let her go. Her skin—golden and toned—feels warm and smooth, droplets of water glisten down her neck and between her breasts, barely secured by her white bikini top. "Let go of me." She kicks under the water, the impact barely noticeable.

"A thank you goes a long way." I hold us there, treading water. She grimaces at me and I smirk. I can do this all fucking day.

"Let. Me. Go!"

"Thank me."

"Thank you for what?"

"For saving you."

"I didn't need saving, but if I did, I hope you'd be the last person around to do so."

"Ouch, you trying to hurt my feelings?"

"Not sure you have any." She wiggles around, trying to wrangle her wrist out of my grip.

I chuckle. I like her like this, with a bit of fire, not just the shy mouse that hides behind overly large suits. When she sheds those, she's a whole other person. The thought startles me, but before I have time to dwell, Emily shoots up then dives down under the water. Her hand, wet and slippery, easily slides from my grip and she disappears beneath the surface and begins to swim to the edge of the pool.

I track her movements and follow above her as she pushes through the water. Her toned muscles ripple with her sure strokes, her long hair trailing behind her in a long, brown waves.

She breaks the surface by the wall and I lunge, trapping her with my body, caging her with my hands, suddenly reluctant to let her go. I've been finding it difficult lately to keep my eyes off her, and to keep my distance. She wriggles but all that happens is that she grinds herself against me. We both feel the reaction my body has to her movements and she freezes, staring up at me.

"Let me go." She hisses as our faces draw perilously close.

"You need to learn some manners."

She huffs and keeps glaring.

"I saved you, you should at least thank me." I lean in against my better judgement, but there's something about her that keeps tugging at me.

"Save me? All you did was interrupt my swim and now you're trying to feed your ego thinking you're some kind of hero."

"I could be your hero." I smirk.

"My hero?"

"Mm-hmm." I like having her this close, her small body wriggling against mine, warming me up in the cold water. My cock pushes against my soaked jeans.

Her eyes burn, her hot breath fans my lips, "Won't your partner get all jealous of you pressed up against a woman? Or are you in an open relationship?"

"My partner?" I frown. "Wolf?"

"Is that his name? Very manly. *He* sounds like a big, strong man. A *real* hero…" She grinds against me, biting her lower lip, "Is that what you like? Is that why you seemed so happy when you thought I had a cock? Does Hunter like to play on both teams?"

"You know perfectly well that I like women." I push into her, my hard, cock grinding against her. She gasps before trying to push me away.

"Do I? It's ok to be a little vulnerable Hunter. Tell me the truth, I won't judge."

"Vulnerability? That's for people like you, not me. And judge all you want, we both know the truth." I don't know why it matters what she thinks of me, or why I want her to want me. She's just another girl in a long line of other forgettable girls.

"People like me? Your arrogance is pathetic."

I scoff, "If I'm so pathetic why did you kiss me the other night?"

"I didn't kiss you, you kissed me."

"You keep thinking that, but we both know what happened. You wanted to kiss me."

She inhales looking like she might slap me before taking me totally by surprise and curling her hand around my neck brushing her fingers through my hair, her long nails dragging along my wet scalp. "You're right," her eyes fall away and lock onto my lips before darting back up to mine, "I did want to kiss you." Her voice is husky and low and my insides flood with desire.

"Well then, I know how you can thank me."

"Oh?" She pushes herself against me and I'm so hard I wonder if she'd let me fuck her right here in the pool. I'd haven't done that before—in daytime hours.

She licks her lips; they glisten in the sun and my cock hurts so good thinking about her sweet, tight pussy.

"A kiss?" She flutters her eyelashes and sucks on her lower lip. I know she's teasing, and I fucking like it. Because as soon as those hot little lips are on mine, I'm going to prove my theory right; she wants me, just like everyone else.

"Mm- hmm." I smile at her and she smiles back. I find myself relaxing, my body wanting to melt into hers.

"What happened to not fraternising with the staff?" Her lips are perilously close to mine.

"This isn't fraternising, it's a thank you for my efforts." I wink at her and my eyes lock on her lush lips. "Anyway, you're off the clock."

Her hands weave through my hair and drag my head backwards instead of forwards, "And you're off your head, I wouldn't kiss you if you were the last man on Earth!" she says a second before her hands leave my hair.

Before I can grasp or react to what she's doing, she

plunges my head under the water and shoots up, using my shoulders as leverage. She slips out of the pool, stands up and walks to her towel. I break the surface, dragging in a long breath before smirking at her. Despite the sudden disappointment that floods me, my cock aches wanting her even more.

She dries off slowly, running her towel in long strokes over her legs and between her breasts, along her neck and over her face before she sashays over to a deck chair where she stretches out without a worry in the world. Her white bikini shows off all her beautiful curves while her dripping hair falls across her shoulders. My gaze follows the droplets as they slink along her glistening skin. I tear my eyes away and suck in a few breaths before pulling myself out of the pool. I rip off my soaked shirt, it's glued to my body like a second skin. I glance over to Emily, who's slipped on her sunglasses. She doesn't turn to look at me and I find it hard to keep my eyes off her.

I shake my head. What the fuck am I doing? I'm still midshift and all the boys have likely seen this exchange. *Fuck*. I stand up and pull off my shoes and socks, then strip off my jeans. They've stuck themselves to me, and I look like a right clown trying to get them off. I stumble and catch myself before putting all my wet clothes in a pile. I spot Daryl still standing by the window, he smirks at me from behind the glass before turning and disappearing somewhere in the house.

I throw another look at Emily. She's still paying me no attention and something like disappointment tugs at me. She looks mad, but she's not acting like she is. She's being indifferent and somehow that feels worse. *Fuck it*. Why do I even care?

I leave her there in her small, sexy fucking bikini on the fucking deck chair with my wet clothes hiding my massive fucking erection.

This day needs to fucking end.

Emily

Water drips down his strong back and tree trunk legs as he trudges away, an annoyed scowl on his face. The cold wind has helped to chill the inferno that's been burning inside me ever since Hunter had me in his arms. His closeness is intoxicating and does things to my body on a molecular level, it wants to devour him. I exhale a few long breaths, cooling my insides. He puts up a cocky front, one that he shows the rest of the world, but I see goodness lurking inside him. It's not just a hero complex, there's so much more that hides behind his stupid pretty face. But he acts like a burn victim—too scared to come near any hot flames. He hides in the shadows just feeling the warmth, but never really revealing himself. I sigh, wishing he'd let me in instead of pushing me away and my stomach drops with a sudden free fall of jealousy at anyone who might be lucky enough to see the parts of him that he hides. I know he's attracted to me in the way that I'm attracted to him, I've seen the way he watches me, I've felt his reactions; but if he thinks for one second I'll fall into his bed cause he flashes me a few smiles and throws a few well-crafted words my way, he has another thing coming. *Right?*

9

***

Hunter

It feels good to be away from work and the smell of coffee filters through the small apartment. I've only been here a handful of times but they've made a few more changes since my last visit. I stare at the framed picture, a shredded illustration that's been pieced back together with clear tape. A half boy, half-wolf stares back at me. The details are astonishing and once again regret filters through me like sand making me feel heavier. Red is so fucking talented. I should have stayed and made sure she went to that art school. She would have been so much happier and more successful; in the same way she would have been with Wolf if I didn't stand in their way.

I think about how in many ways his friendship changed the course of my life. Not so much the trajectory, I was always headed here, but more so that he made things easier. When I saw him that day on the oval darting towards me with fire in his eyes, I didn't think that this giant of a man would turn out to be my best friend; I thought he was going to be the one that ends me. I remember that day so clearly, how he stomped over already much bigger than all the other boys at that stupid school. I already knew what was coming. A battle of egos and a few punches followed by the endless ridicule about the boy whose clothes don't fit properly and were fifth-generation hand-me-downs with the retarded sister.

I hate when they talked about Red like that, but they didn't know how strong she was. How she dealt with all our problems like a champion despite being so young. I remember looking at her and squaring my shoulders, my body tense and ready to fight. I wanted her to see that I'll never back down, that I will always stand up for us and that she will always be safe. Protecting her has been my full-time job since she was a baby. I was never going to let her down.

If Wolf wasn't going to kill me, my chugging heart would have done it instead. It felt like it was going to explode, but I was ready. I've had big fights before and even though I was skinny, I could still hold my own. When he stopped just in front of me with a smirk plastered across his face, I thought then that I would be the one to throw the first punch. But all he wanted was to play ball. It was like he was wearing some kind of glasses that made all my scraggly clothes and appearance disappear. He didn't care at all. That football game changed everything. It was the first time since starting school with all those elite fuckers that I smiled. I had fun.

The thing was, I was sure it would be a one-time thing. So when he showed up the next day and the next, it surprised me. At first, I wondered why a guy like him would want to spend so much time with a loser like me. I was an orphan working two jobs and looking after my sister, while he had everything—money, parents, a future.

Trust was not something I gave out freely. When you get abandoned by your parents and left to fend for yourself, you develop a few issues. They become ingrained in your very bones. They affirm that you are not worth loving and that love is a concept reserved only for the blind and the fools.

But the more I got to know him, the more I realised that he was just as lonely as I was. His parents travelled all the time, and even when they were around, they weren't available to him. He said all his friends were fake and hung around cause they either feared him or wanted something from him. I assured him that he had nothing to worry about, as we weren't friends. He laughed so hard and slapped my back that eventually I followed suit.

After that day, we became more than friends, we were brothers, we were the family we both needed. And even though I was too proud and too blind to accept his help, he helped anyway. Looking back now, I don't know if we would have ever made it without all the "leftovers" he used to bring over and the occasional other perks. Now I have someone who has my back. No matter what. As the years went on, Wolf became a fixture in my life, I could always turn to him now, he was the one person who never let me down. He never left, he never once steered me wrong.

It was a no-brainer that we would go to the same Uni and build our business to be the most successful security firm in London. We always knew we'd have it all, the money, the success, the women—ah… so many, many women.

"Your sister is a genius." Wolf walks into the small lounge with two cups of coffee, pulling me out of my memories and hands me one. He looks good. He has a tan and the fatigue he usually carries with him seems to have released him. The bags under the eyes and the heaviness in his shoulders are gone. He seems almost light, which is strange for a man his size. He's a fucking monster, always has been.

"She is, yes." I nod, taking my coffee from him.

"She said to tell you she'll see you next time you come over."

"So she's still pissed at me?"

He shrugs, "you know what she's like."

I nod, "I do, stubborn."

He chuckles, "She really is." He runs a hand over his face, wiping away a grin. I have a feeling I don't want to know what he might be thinking about. "How's the new gig?"

"Painful. That man's PA is doing my fucking head in."

"His PA?" His eyebrows shoot up and his mouth quirks to one side.

"Yeah. Always getting in the way, being all stubborn and uptight."

"Uptight?" He's fully smiling now.

"Yeah, she just pisses me off all the time." And she does. It really pisses me off that she hasn't cast a single glance my way since the incident in the pool, that she leaves the room any time I walk into it, or that she hasn't offered me a cup of coffee. I'm not sure how I let it happen, but somehow she's gotten under my skin.

Wolf's mouth is stretched in a wide grin that threatens to become full-on laughter. He looks way too amused.

"What?" I snap at him.

"Nothing. Nothing at all," he smirks.

"Wolf."

"Well, when you send me all those messages about Daryl Dark and what a shit he is, I thought he must be a real dick. But now I know the real reason you have your panties in a twist."

"Emily?"

"Is that her name?"

"Oh fuck off, she's just as much a pain in my ass as he is— or as you are, you prick."

"Really? Is that why you haven't mentioned him at all yet?"

"Whatever." I run my hand through my hair and ignore the sudden flush of heat that runs through my body as I think of Emily in her tiny bikini and how her skin felt under my touch. I take a sip of the coffee, wanting to flush the thoughts away. "This tastes like shit." I put my cup down.

Wolf laughs, "It's always tasted this bad; you've been spoiled."

I huff at him. He's probably not wrong, it's not about the coffee anyway.

Wolf leans back into the couch, making it look too small for him. "So, tell me about Saturday night."

<hr>

It's Saturday and I'm grumpy as hell. This morning I had to slink out of some random bed, not wanting to wake the stranger in it. I couldn't remember her name, or what her skin tasted like the night before. Just another girl with a pretty face and a nice pair of tits. Forgettable.

My morning run did nothing for my mood. It's too hot and too humid, and Wolf's words keep ringing in my ears.

I stare at my ceiling, a droplet of water drips from my wet hair and slithers down my back. I need to go but I can't bring myself to move. Daryl is having an event tonight. One that's actually been properly scheduled and planned. He's hired a ballroom in the city and he's invited the who's-who in the industry. Well, those who matter to him. Some kind of preempted celebration of his acceptance into the UK Music Hall of Fame.

I suck in a deep breath and stand, grabbing my keys and heading out the door.

<hr>

The boys are hidden in plain sight as the guests arrive. Primed, perked and prettied beyond recognition. It never ceases to amaze me how much makeup and jewellery these people need to try and hide the fact they are just as ordinary as the rest of us.

I scan the room for the hundredth time. A ballroom in some fancy hotel. There's a dance floor that will eventually be packed with sweaty people, whose makeup will run, hands will rummage around, and saliva will be exchanged. There's a stage at the back where Daryl will be called up to accept his award. Made-up tables with golden painted cutlery surround the rest of the place. It's fancy but fake, much like most of the guests here tonight.

I keep my eyes on Daryl. I can see he's uncomfortable. From the time I've spent with him, I know this isn't his kind of thing, but he's also not stupid. He understands the value of rubbing shoulders with the right people. It's not just his talent that has gotten him this far, it's all about who you know and how many hands you're willing to shake.

My gaze flickers across the room and that's when I spot her. She's wearing a full-length black dress with a long slit up the right side that shows off most of her leg. Her hair has been made, pulled up into a classy bun with curled strands bounding off her back and shoulders, hiding the thin straps of her gown. The dress plunges in the back showing off her naked tanned skin. My fingers itch to run along her back and sink into her hair. She's stunning. And I have a sudden desire to rip that dress off her and make her feel as beautiful as she is.

Rubbing my hands over my face I push the thought away as the music starts and some guy walks up to her. I recognise him as one of Daryl's band members. The bassist. She gives him one of her shy smiles and nods before he takes her hand and leads her to the dance floor. I have a sudden desire to break every bone in his body. Why the fuck is she smiling at a sleaze bag like that?

I spot Wolf; he's eyeing Emily and his gaze darts to mine before his face stretches into a smirk. I'll be sure to wipe that off his face later, right now I can't take my eyes off the bassist's hand which keeps gliding lower and lower towards her ass. Bassists don't really need all of their fingers to play, do they?

Wolf comes over. "How is it looking?" I ask him.

"Quiet." His gaze follows mine and he locks on Emily. He smirks, "Is that her then?"

"Who?"

"The PA?"

"Her name is Emily," I grind out knowing he already knows who she is.

He chuckles, "That's a yes then. I can see why."

"Why what?"

"Why she's so *annoying*." He draws out the last word, and my fists clench by my sides aching to connect with his jaw.

I ignore Wolf and watch as the song ends and the bassist stands too close to her, pulling her into his body. He leans in and whispers in her ear. Her eyes are cast down, and she's wearing that shy smile that makes my cock want to do stupid things to her mouth. Eventually, she shakes her head and pushes away and out of his touch. He looks disappointed and for some reason that makes me incredibly happy.

She looks up and for a second her eyes lock with mine then dart over to Wolf, who gives her one of his trademark smiles. He's being a right dick and I wonder if he'll take any threat about talking to Red seriously.

Daryl comes over and starts blathering on about the night. He's surrounded by people but for some reason, he's decided to talk to me. I smile and nod but I can't hear anything at all as I track Emily.

Wolf has made his way over to her and they're talking. She smiles then covers her mouth as she laughs and my blood runs hot. Their eyes flash over to me and they both laugh again. I'm going to kill Wolf and he knows it as he winks at me.

Daryl follows my gaze and lands on Emily. "Doesn't she look great tonight?"

"Sure, Mr. Dark." I nod and my eyes stay locked on Wolf and Emily.

"Is that one of your men?"

"Yes sir."

"Well, he's a big lad, isn't he? Handsome too. Is he single?"

I shift uncomfortably, wondering where he might be going with this, "No sir, he isn't."

"Pity, they would make a lovely couple. And see how happy he makes her? That's the most I've seen her smile in weeks."

My stomach churns. Maybe she'd smile more if he didn't treat her like such shit. I grind my teeth and nod. *Pity*. Sure, if Wolf was single he'd do more damage to her than anything else. She needs to move away from him. Whatever they are talking about has her smiling and way too comfortable. Wolf catches my stare and grins. He's a fucking dead man.

Daryl slaps me on the back, "Well thanks again, enjoy the night." He's talking to me like he forgets I'm not one of his guests before he turns and walks towards a table of producers.

I take the opportunity and march over to Wolf and Emily. I stare at him and he tips his head before leaving, his face set in a smirk. It needs a readjustment and I promise myself I'd deal with it later.

"What the fuck are you doing?" I glare at her and her smile vanishes. Fuck, why do I have that effect on her?

"I was having a conversation that you rudely interrupted."

"With Wolf?"

"I can talk to whoever I want."

"You can't talk to him."

"Why not? Afraid I'll steal your man?" She throws in my face, and I scowl at her.

I sigh heavily, annoyed she's still taking stupid shots at

me. "He's not my man, he's my sister's man, and he isn't available."

Her face turns a slight shade of red and her nostrils flare. I've obviously said the wrong thing. She opens her mouth to reply but my earpiece crackles to life. The boys outside need two extra bodies, as a few rowdy fans are trying to force their way inside. I spot Wolf already on the move across the room and without a word I turn and bolt towards the door, leaving Emily open-mouthed and furious.

When I get outside I'm greeted by a sea of people. I knew they were here when we snuck in through the back entrance, but it's always confronting seeing so many bodies and listening to the insistent shrieks and cries. It's a tumultuous sea and we're the few lone boats trying to fight the waves.

I spot the two guys straight away. They keep trying to climb over the barricade. Rob and T.K. are keeping them at bay, but with their attention on those guys, a few others are trying to get by. Wolf and I close the distance and I feel the crowd inhale with our presence. We have that effect on people. We extricate the two men from the line and hand them over to the policemen who are there to "oversee things." So far, all I see is them overseeing the female ass in the crowd. I can't say I blame them. There's so much skin on display, it's like walking into a wet dream. But I'm itching to get back inside, where I'm meant to be. That's where I do my job best. At least that's what I keep telling myself as I take the steps two at a time towards the entrance.

"What's the rush?" Wolf follows in my wake.

"They're two men short inside."

"No other reason?"

I swivel around and meet his smirking face. "Stop being such a dick and go do your job."

He chuckles and tips his head towards the packed ballroom where the fucking bassist has his hands all over Emily again. "And who's doing your job?"

Heat simmers below my skin and I resume my post inside the ballroom. Wolf has no idea what he's on about. The guests take their seats and clap as the MC gets onto the stage to introduce Daryl. Emily whispers something into the bassist's ear and he nods. She gets her bag and I watch as he escorts her towards the door.

I'm on them in a few steps. "You're leaving?"

"Yes."

"There's not enough security at the house, let me—"

"She'll be fine mate." The bassist intervenes and I grind my teeth, feeling like they might turn to dust.

"Emily—"

"I'm fine. You should do your job. Here." She turns around and walks away, fuckface in her wake, a smug look on his face.

I want to kill everyone. Slowly.

The ceremony drags on and for some reason, I can't stop looking at my watch. I keep half an eye on Daryl and his cronies. Nothing is happening here. Nothing that concerns me, even though it should. But all I can think about is Emily in that fucking dress and how that bassist ran his fingers on her exposed back and all the ways he must be fucking her right now.

My stomach tightens and I catch Wolf staring at me. He's fucking smirking again. I need this night to end.

We're the last to leave. Daryl wanted to thank everyone fucking personally. Shook hands, smiled slapped backs, kissed cheeks. He's an asshole, but man he knows how to work a crowd when he needs to.

Tom drives the car back to the house like a blind grandmother protecting her cookies and I hold my tongue. If he drives any slower we would be going in reverse. My foot taps the floor of the car and my whole body is humming like I've swallowed a snake pit and they are all slithering and snapping inside me. I need to hit something.

Tom pulls up to the dark house and my stomach tightens thinking of Emily inside. I escort Daryl to the front door, my fists clenched by my sides.

"Want to come in for a nightcap?" he asks and suddenly I'm grateful for his loneliness.

"Sure." We step inside and my gaze flickers to the stairs. The corridor beyond is dark. The house is silent. My stomach knots again.

Daryl strolls through the lounge and grabs a couple of tumblers, chucks some ice in each and pours us a gin. I hate the stuff, the strange lingering taste of juniper mixed with whatever the distiller had in his pantry that day. This one has a hint of lemon behind all the dryness. Daryl doesn't bother with the tonic and lets the entire shot slip down his throat before he grabs himself another. He holds out the bottle in offer and I shake my head. He shrugs.

"It was a great night tonight, wasn't it?"

"Sure thing sir," I say and think about the award he left behind in the back of the car.

"It wears off you know?"

"What does?"

He pours himself a third drink that looks like a double-double and takes a long sip. "All of it."

"Sir?"

"The shine."

I wait for him as he sighs heavily and falls onto the couch, nursing the bottle now.

"I used to love doing this, and I'm fucking good at it. Making music is like breathing, I'll only stop when I die. I used to love everything that came with it." He takes a long swig. "I mean fuck, I love the money and what it affords me —and the pussy. Fuck, I've had more pussy than most men will have in three lifetimes," he chuckles but it's an empty sound. "But here I am, sitting in my big fucking house, with my big fucking dick, talking to you."

I don't know what to say so I remain silent. My neck prickles and I'm way too aware that Emily is somewhere in this house and possibly being fucked by some slimy asshole. I shudder, my hands in tight balls by my sides, my nails digging into my palms.

"Don't go making deals with the devil mate, they leave you soulless." He takes a long sip from his bottle. "The older you get, the more memories you live on; it's hard to make new ones, real ones—and the old ones all blur together into nothingness till you realise you're all fucking alone even when you're surrounded by people. I loathe my own company." He takes a long sip and sighs, sinking further into the couch, "There is too much silence and in my line of work, silence is death, and I can't fucking stand this overbearing solitude."

He stares at the wall for a while, looking every bit his fifty-six years. The lines on his face seemingly deeper and the worry he carries with him etched clearly by the curve of his mouth and droopy eyes. I'm about to ask if he needs anything else before he opens his mouth again.

"I guess I didn't realise how much I'd miss the *real* shit—a real smile, a genuine hug. Something that's not false or forced, something that makes me feel like I'm still alive, like I still really matter beyond my fame and money and music. I want to be someone's whole fucking world again."

I have no idea how to reply to that, so I stay silent staring at the ice in my glass. His eyes glaze over and he lifts them to me, "Go live a little, go make some noise." He waves me away like I'm an annoying fly and takes another long sip from the bottle.

"Good night sir." I put my untouched drink down and he doesn't reply.

In the foyer, I look at the front door then stop. My gaze keeps being drawn to the stairs. Fuck it.

I take them two at a time and rush down the corridor till I

find myself outside her door. Light seeps from beneath and I knock, my fist clenched and irritation sliding across my skin. When there's no answer I knock a little louder.

The door cracks open and Emily's face peeks out. "Hunter?"

I ignore her surprise and push forcefully on the door, driving Emily back before I take a step inside and scan the room. Her bed is empty save for an open laptop and her ruffled duvet.

"What the hell, Hunter?"

Her voice snaps me back to her and my eyes can't help but rake down her body. She's wearing a pink t-shirt that's a few sizes too big. It dips over her naked left shoulder and hovers just above mid-thigh, her long bare legs on display. She's removed her makeup; her hair is loose over her shoulders and she looks like a fucking dessert buffet—all sweet and fucking delicious.

"I asked what you were doing here." Her eyes narrow and she storms past me and to her bed where she snatches a pair of shorts. I don't want her putting them on.

I follow her and snatch the shorts from her hands, throwing them across the room. Her eyes grow wide, then narrow once more. "What the hell are you doing here? Get out!"

It's the third time she's asked and I have no answer—no real one, not one I want to verbalise. What am I doing there? I know exactly what I'm doing in her room at two in the fucking morning. I'm pissed off. At her. And all the things she does even when I shouldn't be. "Just making sure the building is secure and you got home safe."

She scoffs, "I'm not your client, Daryl is. I'm assuming he's fine seeing as you're here."

I nod.

"Great, he's fine, I'm fine, the building is secure. Now

leave." She folds her hands across her chest trying to look tough.

I take a step forward instead, and she backs away from me. "I don't work for you Emily; you need to remember that. Stop telling me how to do my job," I growl.

I take another step and she backs away again, chewing on her bottom lip as she does. "Then leave."

I nod and step forwards again, her back hits the wall, and I move into her space. My hands set on either side of her, caging her in.

"No." I grind out through clenched teeth. I need her to know who she's dealing with, to remember who I am and what I'm capable of. I will not be bossed around by a little elf who thinks she's in charge, who thinks she can just come and go and jeopardise the security of this house. At least it's what I keep telling myself.

"Get. Out." She pushes against my chest, but I don't move. I scoff at her poor effort and grab her hands, pinning them above her head while the rest of me pushes against her, pinning her to the wall. We've been here before.

"Think you're a big man holding down someone half your size?" she sneers at me, "Let go of me and see what I do to you, you coward."

"Coward?" I growl at her, my eyes burning into hers as anger and heat flares inside of me. "You do realize what my job is, don't you? Of course you do. After all, you keep telling me how to do it."

"Being a punching bag or human shield doesn't make you brave, it makes you stupid, especially if you don't give a shit about the person you're taking punches for," she spits out.

"What do you know about it?"

"Bravery is allowing yourself to be vulnerable."

"No, being vulnerable will get you hurt, or killed. Maybe you should stop talking about shit you know nothing about." My hands dig into her wrists and she squirms against me.

My cock feels every movement of her lithe body, and I bite the inside of my cheek.

She shakes her head like we're talking about two different things and maybe we are. Either way, she's being childish and ridiculous.

"You think you're brave?" she growls at me, and her eyes remain locked on mine. They are full of fire and fury.

I release her and her hand comes up in a flurry, I grip it and push it down. Our bodies are an impulse apart, my eyes snap to her lips where she drags her teeth inward over her lip and inhales. The slight movement lights every synapse inside my body and still, all I do is study her. Her round eyes, her soft lips, her heaving chest. We're locked in a checkmate and there are no moves left on the board.

She snatches her wrist from my grip and slams her fists on my chest again. "That's what I thought."

Her scathing remark is like a slap in the face and rage ignites like fire inside me. I grip her chin, forcing her eyes level with mine. They're hot and angry and full of something other than hate. They dart to my mouth a second before her hand slips through my hair and her lips collide with mine. She kisses me. Hard. Forcing her way through the divide of my lips and into my mouth where our tongues meet in a furious dance. The more she pushes into me, the more I want her. My hands close around her hips, gripping her tight body, drawing her in. I need her closer. Her hands run up my back and her fingers dig into my shoulders, finding purchase. She tastes so fucking good, better than I remember. She's so fucking hot pinned against me, and I push harder into her tight, little body.

My hands slide to her ass and she comes up, wrapping her long legs around me like a belt. My hard cock grinds against her and I swallow her moan, making it mine, making her mine. I want to own every fucking inch of her. Her hands rush up into my hair and tug as our mouths remain locked in a frenzied kiss.

I spin and stumble towards the bed while she clings to me. I need her body even closer; I need to feel her warmth. I fall onto the bed, grinding into her while my hand slips under her shirt and I find a bare breast. She moans when I roll the nipple between my thumb and finger but it's not enough. I want to see them, feel them, taste them. Taste her.

I rip the shirt from her and my gaze falls onto her perfect tits. They rise and fall with her breath, her nipples like a dark red wine I just have to taste. My mouth closes around one and she arches her back for me, her nails scratch my back and I bite down. She moans as I graze it with my teeth, pulling and tugging—and still, she presses herself into me, into my mouth.

Fuck. My hand trails along her abdomen and I slide into her underwear. She's fucking soaked. I groan at the feel of her while she grinds into my fingers. I'm so fucking hard. I need more and she needs to learn. I rip her underwear off, stand and pull down my pants and boxers, freeing my cock. I don't wait for her to admire me; cause I don't give a shit. I need to be inside her, to fucking show her. My mouth finds hers again and I kiss her as I line myself up, her heat sending the tip of my cock reeling.

I don't wait, I can't. My mouth falls open as I slam into her and feel her closing around me. Her nails claw at me as I start to pump. Hard. So fucking hard, she throws her head back and makes a sweet little sound I'm going to remember forever. Her hips roll against mine and our bodies smash into each other as I pound into her at a battering pace. I'm lost inside her as I chase my release. Zero control, zero cares, zero fucks—just the feel of her, just proving to her. Fuck her, fuck Emily. And as I think of her name, my body shudders and the orgasm tears through me in a violent thrill that has me seeing stars and groaning hard into her neck.

I remain above her, panting, smelling her skin, her sweet fruity scent and salty sweat. I draw in a shaky breath and pull myself out and away from her. Her eyes are large and round and her mouth slightly open, sucking in small harsh breaths. She looks shell shocked.

Shit.

I feel lost, navigating uncharted territory. I've never lost control like this before, never allowed myself to get totally lost inside another person; but the rage and lust smashed inside me rendering me rampant. I don't even think she came. I pull up my pants, my gaze locked on her face, which remains dismayed. She doesn't move or speak, just breathes, slow shallow breaths that make her stunning little tits move up and down.

I nod like a fucking idiot and slink out of her room like a fucking coward. I close the door and am instantly immersed in the darkness of the hall. My back hits the wall, my eyes squeeze shut.

"Fuck." I hiss through ground teeth.

I sure fucking showed her.

Emily

The door clicks shut. I stare at the ceiling wondering what the fuck just happened. My body burns anywhere he'd touched but my mind is frayed, swinging back and forth like a pendulum. I saw how he looked at me at that party—the jealous undertone of his stance and voice, the way his fists clenched by his side and his eyes burned into me. Pounding at my door, relief flooding his face when he found me alone before he fucked me and left me behind like an afterthought.

I slide off my bed and make my way to the shower where I let the hot water wash away traces of Hunter Evans. I shake my head as the water pelts my scalp and runs down my body.

A wicked tremble sweeps over me as I think about how much I wanted him. I wanted him to fuck me just as he did. But maybe, despite myself, I wanted more, wanted to enjoy it —enjoy him—be with the man who could please three women at once and have them call out his name. Or maybe they were all faking, maybe he's nothing more than a brute and a thug that only cares about himself. A fucking coward. But I've glimpsed another side of him, I know there is so much more hiding behind all the muscle and arrogant facade. I shake my head, confusion settling inside me. I shut the water off and dry myself before sliding into my messy bed. Apart from my crumpled shirt still on the floor and ruined underwear, there's no evidence of him ever being here. I close my eyes and inhale deeply before falling into a restless sleep.

1 0

Emily

He walks into the kitchen looking fresh and pristine as always. I hate that he can do that. My stomach tightens as he approaches then stops. Our eyes lock and he offers me a whispered hello. I look away and keep my gaze trained on my computer screen. I've been sitting here for twenty minutes looking at the contract but my mind doesn't want to absorb any of the information. All I see are squiggly black lines and Hunter's face a second before he kissed me. I shudder.

"I think we should talk," he says and brushes away invisible lint from his shirt.

I stare at his face—his perfect beautiful fucking face and the lips that kissed me last night—and my jaw clenches.

"Nothing to talk about." I shrug and my stomach drops. He fucking walked out, pulled up his pants and left. I shake my head.

"Emily... look..."

"Don't bother," I say and slam my laptop shut, "I get it, you don't fraternise…"

"It's not like—"

"Like I said last night, you're a fucking coward and I'm just fine without you." I step past him and he grabs my elbow, halting my exit.

"I'm trying to—"

"Morning." Hunter's hand drops from my elbow as Daryl walks into the kitchen. He's in his boxers, his fading tattoos on display, his hair a wild mess on his head. His eyes fling from me to Hunter then back again, and a small smile plays on his lips. "Am I interrupting something?"

"No," we say in unison, and I take the opportunity to take a few steps away from Hunter and towards the door.

Daryl's grin spreads wider. "Right then, I'll be ready in an hour. There's a beautiful, young girl in my bed and I need to send her home smiling."

I grimace at the thought and escape the kitchen. I'll speak to Daryl later; I think I'd prefer it if his security detail remained outside the house.

We arrive at the studio and Daryl informs me he wants a closed session. I'll have to stand outside the door and wait. I inhale through clenched teeth.

"If you wanted a closed session, why did you drag me here Daryl? I could be working back at the house; you know you have the upcoming tour—"

"You have a laptop, you can work anywhere, love. I wanted you here, so you're here."

My ears burn red as I feel Hunter's eyes on the back of my neck.

He turns to Hunter, "Be a good lad and grab her that coffee table from inside won't you?"

The silence behind me tells me that Hunter has gone to do what he'd been asked. "Daryl—"

"No, love. No arguments today, just do the fucking job I pay you to do." With that, he turns to leave and enters the studio slamming the door behind him.

Hunter is back a minute later with the small coffee table. He sets it against the wall and leaves for a second time returning with a chair which he pushes under the table.

I look at the table then Hunter, "I'm going to go work in the car."

"You can't." He blocks my way with his huge body as I try to walk off.

"Don't tell me what I can and can't do." I hiss at him trying to move by him.

"Ok." He steps out of my way. and I smirk at my little victory.

I make my way to the parking garage and look around. Tom and the car are gone. *Shit.* I hold my hands over my eyes, my palms digging in, and I inhale deeply before turning back and making my way through the corridor.

Hunter doesn't say a word as I throw my laptop case onto the table and flop into the chair. I pull my laptop from its case and his shadow falls across the table.

"Can we talk?"

"No." I flip the laptop so it faces me.

"Look," he puts his hand over mine and I look up to meet his eyes. "I'm sorry."

"It's fine." I try to rip my hand away but he tightens his grip.

"I don't know what came over me... I'm not usually so— "

"Angry? Selfish? *Fast?*"

His face falls a little, and I know I've hit him where it hurts.

He shrugs, "Ok, I deserve that, but I'm not *that* guy." He

releases my hand and takes a small step back. "You made me lose control."

"So, it's my fault?"

"Fuck." He whispers and shakes his head, "That's not what I mean. There's just something about you that pisses me off."

"Right."

"No, in a good way."

What the fuck does that mean? "Ok, if you say so." My heart feels like a deflating balloon, the air painfully and slowly bleeding out till all that's left is a hollow, limp sack.

"Emily—"

"Just forget about it, Hunter. Free pass—it never happened." I open my laptop and glue my eyes to the screen, clenching my jaw and praying the tears that flood my eyes won't spill onto my face.

Hunter

I stare at the mansion's closed front door. I've felt on edge all morning and nothing, not my run, my workout, or a quick rub and tug has settled my mood. All I can think about is Emily's face dropping when I told her she pisses me off and her tone when she accused me of being too selfish and too fast. I know it wasn't my best performance, but I know she enjoyed it. Enjoyed me.

All I can do is breathe and wait. Emily has talked Daryl into keeping me outside like a dog. Tom kept his mouth shut despite the amusement etched across his face. Just three weeks to go and this nightmare will be over.

The door creaks open and Daryl steps out, unsurprising he's not ready and his boxers hang loosely around his skinny frame. He pushes Emily forwards. She's in one of her dark grey suits again. She looks like a tombstone.

"Morning." He flashes his teeth and tucks his wild hair behind his ears. "Izabel has arrived, I need you to go pick her up for me. Guard her with your life."

I look at the man as if he has lost his mind. He does know I'm not his errand boy. "I'm sorry sir, but my job is to protect you, I can't leave the—"

"Your job today is to get Izabel home to me in one piece. Without her, I'm a dead man anyway."

"Sir I—"

"No need to fret. I'm surrounded by a bunch of guys who look like they hunt and eat grizzly bears for breakfast, I'll be fine. I need you to make sure my Izabel gets to me safely."

"But sir—"

"Emily here has all the paperwork for her release," he pats her on the shoulder, "don't you, love?"

She twists out of his grasp and nods stiffly.

"Can you take your car? I need Tom."

"Sir—"

"Great." He smiles at me, then gives me a long meaningful look "With. Your. Life." He lets the words hang in the air for a second before he swivels back into the house shutting the door behind him.

- - -

Irritation crawls along my body and I press the unlock button a little more violently than necessary and get in slamming the door behind me. I grip my steering wheel and wait for Emily to get in. She leans against the window not looking at me like she'd rather be anywhere else in the world than here. The feeling is mutual.

I turn on the car and we sit, the engine idles, purring beneath us. I turn and look at her. When we haven't moved for a few minutes, she turns and glares, "Can we go?" she bites out.

"I'm not leaving till I know who Izabel is, I'm not putting some random in my car and bringing her back here without doing background checks and getting them a security clearance."

Emily's face splits into a sardonic smile. "She's his guitar."

"A fucking guitar?" I hiss and my grip tightens on the steering wheel, painting my knuckles white.

She nods and turns back to the window, keeping her gaze firmly fixed on a cloud.

I grind my teeth and pull away, my tyres screech as I do, and I can hear the boys' laughter in my mind's eye. When Wolf gets wind of this I'll never fucking live it down. I put my foot down tearing through the morning traffic.

Some city DJ rambles on, seems he's excited about the "Drowning in Darkness" tour and Daryl's new album. "Twisted Heartstrings" blares from the radio, his most famous song, the one that propelled him to the top of the charts and cemented him as a rock legend.

"Why the fuck is this guitar so important?" I snap at Emily and she jumps at the sound of my voice, irritated that she hasn't said a word in almost twenty minutes, that I'm a fucking driver for the day and a fucking delivery boy. This isn't in my fucking job description.

"It's not just any guitar," she says and sighs. She almost sounds nostalgic.

"Why is it so important to him?" For the first time since we left the house she faces me then settles into her seat, her head falling back, her eyes fixed on the ceiling.

"Izabel was the love of Daryl's life."

"Was?"

She gives me a small nod, "Before he was who he is today, before he was Daryl Dark and lost his soul, she was his everything."

I wait because I want to know more and I know how people love to fill silences with words. They can't help it. And right on cue, she does.

"He met her when he was eighteen, when he took a vacation to Mexico with some friends. I don't know the specifics but I know he went out dancing and spotted her from across the room. He said she was like a planet and he gravitated towards her. He couldn't help the pull she had on him. He said it felt like being lost but in the right direction. And once she fell into his arms, he couldn't let her go." Her eyes glaze over like she is lost in the story.

"He spent his entire two weeks lost with her, in her. He said she was mysterious and mischievous and he'd wake up each morning wondering what was going to happen next.

If you ask him, he describes himself as stupidly naive. Like all eighteen-year-olds, he was so sure of himself. Careless. Arrogant. Believing himself to be indestructible, which is why falling in love with Izabel so crushingly and devastatingly was disturbing and maddening. It stripped away all his fake sense of security and left him vulnerable and exposed in a way he'd never imagined.

When his holiday was near its end, he said the mere thought of leaving her behind left him agonised. He needed her to soothe the ache he felt when she wasn't near him. He could not bear to be without her, knowing all his days would be full of constant and relentless thoughts of her. And maybe it was selfish to pluck her from her world, the one that made her, the one which fed her spirit and creativity and desires, but he did.

He promised her the world. He brought her back to the UK. He was infatuated, mesmerized, besotted with her; and she inspired him. The few who knew her said she had the power to make him gravitate to her in a room full of people. She was the centre of his universe and he revolved around her."

She stops for a minute and takes in a long breath as if the story is taking a toll on her, then continues. "It was about that time that he got picked up with his single "In the Dark." Many people think it's a tragic song, but it's a celebration of his love for her. He wrote it for her, she inspired him. In fact, his first album "Towards the Light" was all about them. If you listen to the lyrics, *really* listen, you can tell how much he loved her because *after*, nothing ever sounds the same."

"After?" I can't help myself; she's drawn me into her story and now I need to know. The airport comes into view and I make a right towards the short-term parking.

"Daryl had a friend, the best of friends, and they grew up together. Their careers took off at the same time, and the three of them were inseparable until one night, Izabel chose his best friend's bed over his." Emily chews on her lower lip and clears her throat. "Everyone said that after that day, his heart stopped working properly. He's a fallen star with nothing to orbit around, fated to drift alone through space forever."

"That's a bit dramatic."

She shrugs, the fog that covered her eyes fades as she comes back to the car, and I know I've ruined it for her. But fuck it, all this romance is making me a little queasy. "It's what being in love feels like. It tears at your heart slowly and painfully until it either completes you or leaves a permanent hole."

"Sounds painful."

"It's meant to be."

"Really? That's not what the books say."

She scoffs, "You read?"

"Of course."

Her eyes widened a little as if I caught her by surprise, and I like that she sees this part of me; I'm more than what she assumes. Than what everyone assumes. She shifts in her seat and schools her face. "What do you like reading?"

"Lots of different things, philosophy, history, the classics. I like to strengthen my mind through knowledge."

"And what about your heart?"

"It's a vital organ with four chambers whose sole purpose is to pump blood through the body."

She doesn't answer for a while then turns back to the window as I search for a parking spot. "Being in love is the best and worst feeling all smashed together. It bubbles around like some kind of mad experiment gone right or wrong. If it endures, it tastes sweet. But if it ends, it leaves a sour aftertaste."

"It always ends." I find a spot and swing my arm behind her headrest as I begin reverse parking.

"It doesn't."

"It ended for Daryl."

"But that's just the thing, it hasn't."

I park, turn off the engine and turn to Emily, "She's left him for someone else."

"Yes." She draws in a long breath as if she's feeling the pain of Izabel's absence as her own. "'*Twisted Heartstrings*' was the last song he wrote before he named his guitar and hasn't touched it since. He wrote it for Izabel. A true love song. It's a declaration that his love for her is real and enduring. It's a promise that she's worth waiting for. He will wait until the end of time and find his orbit once again."

"It sounds doomed."

"Even doomed love is worth feeling."

"Why? It breaks you."

She doesn't answer, just shakes her head as If I'm missing something vital, then opens her door and steps outside. I follow her to the elevator that takes us into the terminal building.

Her flat sensible shoes don't make a sound as she weaves through the terminal and makes her way to a side door. It's white like the wall and almost invisible.

She knocks. The door opens and a man in a navy-blue cardigan opens the door. He's no more than forty and his stomach hangs over his too-tight pants. A light smear of something that could have been mayonnaise clings to the edge of his beard. Emily greets him and his gaze tracks her body. When he sees nothing other than a rectangular shape he zeros in on her face.

"Can I help you?"

"Yes, I'm here to pick up a package." She schools her face and shoves the paperwork towards the man who takes it from her. The papers ruffle in his hand as he reads through the pile, then ushers us inside and into his cramped office. Much like its owner, it seems to be bursting through the seams. The desk is crammed with files and discarded candy wrappers, an overflowing bin and the smell of onions covered up by artificial floral scents. The place is sad, decrepit and makes me wonder if that's what giving up on life looks like.

"Sit, please." He gestures to two chairs at the edge of his desk, "I'll just go to the back and retrieve it for you."

Emily doesn't move. She remains just inside the door and folds her arms in front of her chest.

"Suit yourself." He shrugs and lumbers down the narrow corridor.

We wait in a long silence. Emily keeps checking her nails and fidgeting. I make her uncomfortable.

"You didn't answer my question." I break our silence and her eyes find mine.

"Which one?"

"About doomed love, what's the point?"

She draws in a long breath and her hazel eyes study mine

like she's searching for something, "Have you ever been in love Hunter?"

The question takes me by surprise, so I give her my typical go-to answer. "Of course not, love is just a transient feeling of happiness, it's not something that lingers. It's a made-up thing girls tell you to try and keep you around."

"You really believe that?"

"Sure," I say and watch as her mouth twitches a little, her pretty lips pointing downwards. I seem to keep having that effect on her.

"Well then, you won't understand anyway." Her eyes drop from mine and she studies her fingers again.

I'm about to ask her to explain it anyway when the man plods back through the corridor, empty-handed. His red face is covered in a sheen of sweat and the mayonnaise has vanished from his beard. He comes to a stop in front of us and pants slightly. "This may take longer than I thought."

"What do you mean?"

"I mean we've misplaced the item."

"Misplaced?" The colour drains from her face but her back remains straight and her features sharp.

"It will just take a little longer to locate than I thought is all." He gets defensive, his eyes flash from Emily to me.

"How much longer?" I ask and get a quick sharp look from Emily.

"Can't be sure, just take a seat." He points to the chairs again. I wait for Emily; she remains in place and the man shrugs.

"Suit yourself, just thought you should know." He turns away and leaves us rooted to the spot. As if on cue, Emily's phone rings, Daryl's name flashes across the screen. She silences the phone and tucks it into her pocket.

"You ok?"

"Why wouldn't I be?"

She's defensive and irritated. I put my hands up in

surrender and her eyes fall away again. The silence presses against us making the smell of onions rise to the surface.

"You've really never been in love?" Her voice sounds too loud in the empty room.

"No." I shrug.

"But you've been with women?"

"I have been with a lot of women, yes, but haven't dated them if that's what you're asking." I bite down the smirk that wants to curl on my lips, somehow it doesn't feel appropriate.

"But why?"

"Why? I don't know. First, there was my sister and then the job—late nights and long hours, weeks away from home —I guess I'm just not dating material."

"So, you just fuck random women?"

I shrug. I'm pretty sure she already knows the answer to that.

"Like we did?"

Oh. I rub my hands over my face and try to find her eyes. "No, not like we did. That was a first for me."

One of her eyebrows arch up and she's asking me for more. I search my brain for the right words not knowing if I could articulate the answer she wants.

"It's not usually like that or that fast." There. Saved it, and hopefully regained part of my dignity.

"Right." Her lips pinch and I know I didn't give her the answer she was looking for. "Is it because I piss you off?"

Shit. I forgot that I told her that. "No. Maybe." I sigh feeling like I've just twisted myself into a too-tight knot and there's no undoing what I did. "Something was different with you."

"Different how?" She doesn't relent and I know I have to give her something or she'll keep questioning me. Maybe she does deserve the truth or some version of it.

"I just lost control. It's not something that has never happened to me before. With women. Ever."

Her face twists and I know she's considering my words. I'm not sure if they hurt her. They weren't meant to. I just can't tell her that my anger flared into passion, that she pisses me off for all the wrong reasons, because maybe I do like being around her. Maybe I think she's kind and funny and interesting. She makes my temper rise over stupid shit, and I can't explain why. I can't explain why I lost it when I saw her with Wolf, even though I knew he'd never touch her. There's so much about the way she makes me feel when I'm around that I can't explain. But the worst thing of all, is that I can't explain why I fucking like it and how much I fucking liked being inside her.

"Look, I'm sorry…" I start but she cuts me off.

"What did I do?"

"What?"

"That day, what did I do?"

I rub my hands together feeling the room shrink around me, and as I formulate a reply, the man returns once again. I notice he's still empty-handed, but I don't care. He's bought me the time I need to divert our conversation. He comes to face Emily, his brow peppered in sweat.

"Where is my guitar?" She asks, and the man looks from her to me to the paperwork and back again, like maybe he thinks one of us has the answers.

"I'm sorry, we just can't locate it." One of the sweat beads on his brow gives up and starts a long slick descend along his cheek. He wipes it away and his sleeve comes back wet. He tucks it behind his back as I hold back a grimace.

"Go look again."

"We've already looked."

"So look again." She says, her jaw tightens and she glares at the man. He takes a step backwards. For a tiny pixy, she can be scary. I keep my features neutral, holding back a smile.

The many layers of Emily. I'm enjoying watching them peel away in front of me. The thought makes my cock jerk in my pants and I realise those are not the only layers of Emily I like to see coming off. I bat the thoughts away and tune back into their staring match deciding to join in. I take a tiny step forward and give him a meaningful look. He understands it perfectly. His shoulders drop and his eyes fall to the ground.

"I'll take another look." He says, his voice drenched in defeat, before he turns away and leaves for a third time.

"You and Red have a lot in common," I say. A diversion tactic, but also the truth. "She's fiery and resilient, just like you."

"Did she piss you off too?"

Oh shit. So much for diversions. "All the time, although she's the one that's not talking to me right now."

"Oh?"

"It's a long story."

"I think we have time." She looks around the deserted office and dim corridor before her gaze swings back to me.

I sigh. Resigned. "I stood in the way of something she wanted." I give her the short version.

Her brows draw together, "Why?"

I grip the back of my neck and search the ceiling. *Why? Such a loaded question.* "Because I thought I was doing what was best for her."

"You were protecting her?"

"I thought I was. Turns out I was wrong," I say on a sigh, and her face changes like she sees something that wasn't there before.

"You? Wrong? What a shock," she scoffs at me.

"Careful," I warn her.

"You don't give much away, do you? What else are you hiding behind that beautiful face of yours?"

My eyebrows shoot up and my lips quirk on a slight smile, "You think I have a beautiful face?"

Her eyes bulge and pink rushes to her cheeks like she's realised that she's let her thoughts slide out. "I mean, I just wonder what you're really like, on the inside, everything you keep inside yourself. You're not...." She shakes her head and bites her lower lip; her shoulders sink and she's never looked fucking sexier.

A million responses start to form inside my mind when once again we are interrupted. Emily ignores Daryl's call again as the man shuffles back into the room. His cardigan is gone and his face is flushed.

He looks sheepish as he turns to Emily, "I'm sorry miss, we can't locate your item."

"I'd like to speak to a supervisor." Her shoulders square as she turns a shade of grey.

The man clears his throat. "He's out."

"And when will he be back?"

"I'm not sure, but—"

"Who can I speak to?" her voice rises in pitch.

The man shuffles under her glare. "Look, we have your details. We will keep looking, and I'll call you as soon as we locate it."

"I'm not leaving here without it." She folds her arms across her chest and roots herself into the spot.

The man studies her, seemingly lost.

"Emily." She swirls to look at me and it looks like she's about to strike out like a coiled angry viper. "Let's go get something to eat, we can come back in an hour?"

Her nostrils flare as she draws in a few breaths then finally tips her head. The man looks relieved. I don't know why. I haven't finished dealing with him yet. He just doesn't know it. He puts his keycard to the door; it beeps and he pushes it open. We exit the small room and I inhale deeply.

The smell of humanity, perfume and coffee is almost refreshing.

Emily doesn't stand around, she trudges through the terminal looking for a place to wait when a skeletal man with sharp, serpentine features jumps up from a seat, a camera in his hand. "Emilia?" He calls out.

Emily looks startled as she looks directly at the man who snaps a picture of her. She surges ahead as the man begins to run after us, I block his way while his camera keeps snapping constantly. *What the fuck?*

Emily spots the business lounge and rushes towards it, she produces a card of some kind and we're let in, leaving the man behind us. I can still hear him calling for Emilia.

The lounge is too bright with floor to ceiling windows, and everything is covered in white. It's blinding and uncomfortable. Classical music plays in the background mingling with the low hum of murmured conversations.

I scan the room and find an empty table in the back. It's shaded and out of the way, I point it out to Emily, she's spotted it too and already weaving her way towards it.

She falls into one of the chairs and leans back, her jaw tight, her hands clutched in little fists which rest on her thigh. I slide in next to her and wait.

"What was that?"

"Nothing. The paparazzi know me as Daryl's PA and he saw you. He must have thought Daryl was here…"

"He called you Emilia."

"It's easy to confuse my name, I'm a nobody."

"You're not." Her eyes find mine and hold them.

Her phone rings again, breaking the moment and she ignores it, then drags a hand over her face. When she looks up, whatever I saw in her eyes a second ago is gone, "Can you get me a drink?"

Emily

He looks a little surprised but covers it up well, then gets up and goes to order the vodka mixer I asked for. So what if it's not even noon? I need some liquid courage if I'm going to tell Daryl Izabel is missing. I know what that guitar means to him, losing her would be like losing Izabel all over again. I lace and unlace my hands, that bloody paparazzi out there has me a little rattled. The last thing I need is to get recognised.

I glare at my phone. Five missed calls. I've never ignored him. Not once since I started working for him. Not at two am when he needed a lift home from some party and didn't even know where he was, not during my birthday dinner when he needed me to buy that mustang he had an eye on, not even when I was at my best friend's wedding and he called midway through the ceremony to ask me if I'd remembered to make sure I asked the hotel staff to only have the blue smarties in his room. I shake my head and sigh just as a glass lands in my periphery.

Hunter slides into the seat next to mine and I snatch a look at his perfect face - he has a face to fall in love with. I know I should be worried about Daryl and Izabel but all I can think about is him with all the other women he spoke about and it feels like a knife twists inside me. Why do they get to have more of him and I get to taste his anger?

I piss him off. But I don't want to.

"Thank you." I grab my drink and sip. The alcohol burns its way down my throat and warms my insides.

He watches me intently and his stare slides under my skin till every inch of me feels like I'm on fire. It hurts. I shuffle in my seat wanting him to stop, needing space because I know every second I spend with Hunter is a second too long, a second that will end up burning me alive. I'm already in free-fall, and I want his arms to catch me. But I know all that waits at the bottom of the abyss is darkness and pain as I shatter.

I down my drink wanting to douse the fire that burns inside me. Dull the pain of want and desire. "Get me another one."

He quirks an eyebrow but says nothing as he gets up towards the bar. I shouldn't admire his broad sloping shoulders and strong back and the way his ass looks in his jeans as he walks through the place like he fucking owns it. I like the way men look at him, with slight trepidation, like they know their place around him, while I hate the way the women look at him like they want to be owned by him. I shove the thought away.

My second drink goes down just as quickly as the first.

"Another please."

"Maybe you should slow down?"

"Maybe you should just do your fucking job."

"Fetching your drinks isn't in my job description," he leans in so close that his breath fans my mouth as his eyes hold mine, "I'm not your fucking errand boy."

He's pissed off—again—and a quake rumbles inside me. He's so close I can smell his shampoo and his body wash, spicy and fresh with a hint of sweat. "Fine then."

I get up and push by him and get myself a double. I slide back into the seat opposite him and smirk at him as I down my drink.

"We're leaving." He stands as soon as my glass is empty.

"No, we're not. I'm still waiting for them to call me back and I'm not leaving this place without Izabel."

Hunter leans over me, his broad body towering over me, his face almost menacing as it lands an inch from mine, setting my heart on a rampage, "You are going to stand up and walk with me to the car, or I'm going to pick you up, throw you over my shoulder, and march out of here with you kicking and screaming."

"You wouldn't dare!"

"Try me." He growls in my face and somewhere inside me I feel a deep tremor as I picture his strong arms snake around me and throw me over his shoulder. I swallow the lump in my throat.

"Fine!" I stand up and feel the alcohol sink to my feet then shoot through my body, warming me up. Or maybe it's the intensity of his glare as he stares into my eyes. The green in his darken like a forest in a thunderstorm.

I shake my head, breaking eye contact. Maybe I did drink too much too quickly. I don't want to go out through the front door again, what if the photographer is still out there? He recognised me, despite everything. He's going to sell whatever picture he manages to snap and my face will be splattered across every tabloid in the country tomorrow morning. I sigh.

"That guy will be waiting for us out there." I try to sound as matter-of-factly as I can even as my heart whips against my chest.

"I'll take care of it," he says, oozing confidence and nonchalance. Then again, it is his job. Finally, he might come in handy.

Hunter follows me out of the lounge, and as expected, the weasel is waiting with his camera in hand, eyes full of dollar signs—*fuck.*

"Emilia, Emilia look here, let me take a picture of you." I hear the snap of his camera as I look down and cover my face. If Hunter doesn't deal with this guy, I'll have to call my dad's publicist and it will get back to him—and that's the last thing I want. I walk faster.

"Emilia." The guy calls again. People are starting to stare and I need to make an exit.

Hunter leaves my side and the man is no longer shouting my name. I chance a backwards glance and see Hunter has him pinned against a wall with one large hand the other wrapped around his camera. He leans in and starts whispering in the photographer's ear and his face drains of colour. When Hunter pulls back, the man is nodding frantically and starts playing with his camera. Both he and Hunter watch the screen. Hunter nods and says something which has the man nodding again before Hunter releases him. The man walks backwards till he's put enough distance between Hunter and himself then turns and walks in the opposite direction, not giving me another glance.

Hunter saunters over to me, a smug smile plastered across his face, "Shall we go?"

I grind my teeth and follow him. "What did you tell him?"

"I told him he can't publish pictures of my ass without my permission and that he should leave us alone." He winks at me and I battle a smile.

We make it to the car. Adrenaline surges inside me wiping away the alcohol. I slam the car door and my phone buzzes again. Hunter gives me a sidelong look as he starts the engine. "You gonna get that?"

I shake my head and silence the phone. "I can't... I can't face him yet; I need more time." More time to gather my thoughts and my courage and maybe my things. I make a mental note of everything I've learned, all my contacts and plans. I guess I can move them forward.

Leap.

"You want me to take you somewhere?"

His kindness makes my heart swell and I wish it wouldn't. "I have nowhere to go." It's true. I've tried to remain mostly anonymous while I've been here—staying in the house, only going to the studio and back, being out only when needed, hiding in plain sight. But today shook me. If that guy recognised me, how long will it be till others do too?

"I know a place." He winks at me and it sends a long, warm shiver down my body. I nod and he drives out of the parking garage.

11

Hunter

I had no intentions of bringing her here. In fact, if Wolf was still living with me, he'd wring my neck. We had just two rules for this apartment and I've just broken the first. Never bring a girl over. No matter how pretty or sweet or how much we wanted to fuck her, there should always be an alternative—starting with her place and ending in the hotel a few blocks down the road where I basically have a membership to room 675.

I park the car and step out, letting Emily follow me up the stairs and hold the door open for her. Since Red and Wolf moved out, the place could use a bit of love. If she notices, she keeps her thoughts to herself as she scans the space and makes her way to the couch.

"New paint job?"

Nothing gets past her. "Yeah." If only she knew why she might not be too excited about it. Seems it's easier to sand over blood stains and paint the wall than to try and clean it.

Problem is, when you paint one spot the rest of the dirt glares at you, so you have to paint the rest. Fucking Jenny. My eyes snap up at Emily, and for a second, I hope I haven't made a dire mistake.

"Coffee?"

"Sure." She gives me a tight smile as she scans the room, I leave her to it while I make the drinks.

When I come back she's standing at the mantle, her fingers lightly brush the framed picture of the three of us. I'm sure she recognises Wolf.

"Is that your sister?"

"No he is far too ugly and a man, the other one is though." I try to break some of the tension between us. I think I see her lips twitch in a smile. I hand over her coffee.

"Thanks. She's pretty."

"I guess so." I shrug.

"Where is she now?"

"Probably at home or at the gallery."

"She's an artist?" her face lights up a little.

"Yeah, a really good one." I feel the pride swell in my chest. Red worked so fucking hard to get where she did. She deserves all that success. Fuck. I really do need to tell her that. If she ever speaks to me again. "You guys look happy."

I feel the smile tugging at my lips remembering that day. "We were."

"And now?"

I sigh, "Now? She's with Wolf and I need to make amends."

"She's punishing you?"

"I deserve it." I don't elaborate and I'm thankful she doesn't pry; it still feels pretty raw. I know what I did was wrong but it all came from a good place and Red holding it against me, despite everything I've done for her over the years, stings. But she can't be coaxed and pushed, when she's ready we will have that conversation.

"What will you tell Daryl?" I divert.

Her brows furrow and she drags her fingers slowly over her lips as she thinks. "I don't know yet," she takes a long sip, "thanks for bringing me here."

"It's fine."

"No, really, I appreciate it. Especially because..." she shakes her head and stops talking, pink colouring her cheeks.

I take a step closer, "Because?"

She shakes her head again and the pink deepens.

I take another step closer and grab her chin, coaxing it up so that her eyes meet mine, "Because?"

She draws in a long breath as if defeated, "Because I'm not sure you even like me."

I frown. But then I think about all our previous interactions and my stomach squeezes. I can see why she might think that. "That's not true. There're a lot of things I like about you."

"There are?" Her voice is a quiet whisper.

"Sure. The way you handle Daryl even when he treats you like shit, the way you carry yourself in a room, you're smart and funny and very talented." Her mouth parts just a little and my body heats up. I've said too much.

I should step away and offer to take her back, but I can't move. I'm rooted in place, searching her hazel eyes, watching the caramel swirl inside as it heats. We had our moment; I've already fucked her. The next guy she meets can be the one that makes love to her. It's what she wants. I can tell.

But the thought of another man inside her makes my body tight and my skin crawl. I don't want her to remember me as the man that fucked her. She called me selfish and fast. I'm neither of those things. I know what pleasure is, and maybe I could give it to her, maybe I could erase that memory for her and replace it with a better one. I can do that —for *her*.

I barely notice myself getting closer to her, staring down

at her, kissing her. It's a soft kiss, a gentle kiss. I can be gentle, I can be caring—for her—I could, to show her I can be. She doesn't back away. Instead, her hands snake around my neck in invitation and my arms wrap around her, pulling her flush against me.

My hand finds its way into her hair and I tug lightly, kissing her harder this time, my tongue slips into her mouth and I taste her again. A lethal combination of coffee and Emily. I fasten her to me, wanting more—convincing myself that all I'm doing is wanting to give *her* more, a better memory. I'm loath to break the kiss, and when I do, she whimpers. She wants this.

I lace my hand through hers and lead her to my bedroom. She sits on the edge of my bed where I can finally kiss her again, touch her, and take my time to explore her. I loom over her forcing her back onto the bed where I tuck myself between her legs and kiss her as I grind my hard cock into her. She moans into my mouth and I swallow the sound making it mine. Today I'm going to make everything about her mine.

My hands slide beneath her shirt, her skin is heated and soft and I find her breast. I tease the nipple over the fabric and she arches into me, whimpering as I kiss her jaw and drag my teeth over her neck. But I want more, I want every-thing—for *her*.

I break the kiss and lift her shirt; she lets me remove it then goes for mine. I'm more than happy to oblige, my skin craves hers. I allow her a short moment to take me in, her eyes rake over my torso before I reach behind her and unclasp her bra. I want to see her, a pleasure I didn't get to enjoy during our previous encounter.

I unzip her skirt and remove it, along with her under-wear, then take a minute to relish in a naked Emily. She's fucking perfect. Her swollen glistening lips are parted and her beautiful breasts rise and fall with her sharp breaths. Her hip bones jut out slightly and her tightly squeezed thighs hide her sweet pussy. But I'm not worried, I plan on getting very well acquainted with it.

I kiss her. Kissing her could be my full-time job, and I would die a happy man. But I don't just kiss her lips, every inch of her screams for my attention—her long neck, her collar bones, her dark rosy nipple, that tighten in my mouth and every time my thumb rolls over them. Fuck, she tastes so good. I kiss her hips and the thin pink circumference left by her underwear, then back up again. She mewls like she was expecting more and I smile against her belly button.

I will make her suffer with pleasure till every other man she thinks about will be nothing but a disappointment.

My mouth closes around a nipple and she arches into me, a muffled moan rips from her lips and I find the other with my hand, teasing it till she whimpers and presses harder into me. I'm so fucking hard and so fucking ready, but I still haven't shown her everything. My hand slides down her belly and between her legs where I find her wet, hot pussy. I run my fingers up and down, a gentle touch that has her whimpering and her hips rolling.

Fuck, she's pretty when she wants me, when she wants more; but I also want more of Emily, I want to know what every inch of her tastes like. I kiss the contours of her hips and that place where her hip bones dip and she wriggles under my kisses. I kiss her toned thighs then inside them, and when I think she has suffered through enough frustration I take my first taste of her. A sweet, little sound rips from her mouth and floods my senses. Fuck, everything about her is delicious. My tongue teases and licks while my eyes are locked to her face. I want to see it when she cums. I don't want to miss a breath, a frown, a single facial expression.

Her head whips back into my pillow and she bites down hard on her lower lip. Her hips grind against my tongue and her body begins to shake and tighten. Her thighs lock around my head, her breath comes out in short, harsh pants. She mumbles—it could be a prayer, or maybe she is begging—it sounds desperate and beautiful and I run my hands up to her breast where I tug on her nipples. Her thighs clamp around me and her fingers claw at my scalp as she cries out to God and I smirk against her hot, wet pussy as she grinds it into my mouth.

Her body slackens and I take a second to rip off my clothes before I slowly crawl up her body. I'm not done yet, and I'm so hard it hurts. I kiss her everywhere on the way up —her skin coated in a sheen of sweat—till I find her mouth and catch her lips with mine. I line myself up with her, her heat alone threatening to push me over.

With a slow long thrust, I'm inside her and her wet heat overwhelms my senses. My pulse drums against my throat as I move inside her, finding respite in her lips. I keep my pace slow, hitting her sensitive clit. Her hips roll against me, and I grit my teeth. I want to last, I want to see her face again, this time from close up. I want to hear the words she mumbles. Her legs wrap around me and her head falls back, framed by her lush thick hair. My hands move down to her ass and I quicken my pace, lust coils inside my body, and I need release.

She cries out again, and fuck, I love that sound. It speaks to the beast inside me that starts to pound against her, hard sharp thrusts that hit her clit. She shakes beneath me, mumbling, talking to the gods again. My mouth closes around her nipple, sending her over. "Fuck Hunter." She cries as she clings to me, fingers clawing at my back, hips pushing against mine and her pussy squeezes me so tightly, my orgasm shatters across my body. I bury my face in her nape and cum hard—harder than I remember coming in a long time. I push myself deep into her and let go.

Her face nuzzles on my chest and I relish in her scent and the feel of her. I don't entirely know what it is about her that makes me feel so content.

"Do you ever get scared?" her voice is silky and tired and her question surprises me, like so many of her previous ones.

"Nah."

"Really?" she lifts up and looks into my eyes.

I shrug. "When you get into it, if it comes to that, when you're making sure you or your client don't get hurt, you're full of adrenalin and too busy fighting to really think about it."

She nods and her head tilts a little, "and after?"

I exhale slowly, "not scared, but sometimes you run other scenarios in your head, like how things could have ended up. But I don't dwell on it. Fear had no place in this line of work."

"Cause you're so tough?"

I grunt, "No, cause I try to be smart. I learned that early. I had to win, but I also had to come out of it as best as I could if I didn't."

"When you were a kid?"

I nod.

"What was that like?"

I sigh and tuck an errant hair behind her ear. "I did what I had to do."

"You must have been scared then."

I shake my head wondering if I was. "I think I was too busy being hungry and looking after Red. Other kids picked on me cause they thought being poor and orphaned made me an easy target, but they soon learned to leave me alone."

"It must have been so hard for you." Her voice is so caring and intimate, it thrums through my body.

I shift a little not wanting to talk about it. That past is gone. That kid is gone, and I don't need anyone's pity or sympathy. I do the thing I do best and divert the conversation. "What about you?"

"Me?" Her eyes fall away and her fingers trace a long line along my abdomen.

"Your childhood, your parents."

"My dad travelled a lot with his business so I didn't get to spend much time with him growing up."

I recall something about Mr. Shepard being a businessman. "And your mom?"

She bites on her lip and looks away, staying quiet for a moment. "I lived with her; she was a great mom."

"Was?"

Her lips twitch and bend in that way they do when they try to hold back pain, "Before she died, she told me that she and my dad were tragically in love in the worst possible way."

"What does that mean?"

She shrugs and doesn't elaborate. She knows a little about the pain of losing a parent. I don't peel away at that question just now; I know how much it hurts. I go a different angle. I want to keep making her smile for just a little longer. "Is that what you want?"

"To be tragically in love?"

I nod.

"It would be an incredible adventure."

"A tragic adventure?"

"A beautiful one."

I purse my lips in a strange half-smile half frown, "I'm sure you'll find it one day."

"One day." She smiles and her eyes shimmer like she sees something on my face that's not there, and my words lodge in my throat as my heart chugs. No. I don't do love, tragic or otherwise. Whatever she is thinking needs to be extinguished, and quickly.

"Well 'one day' isn't on my calendar."

Her smile fades and my stomach coils, hating that I've made her feel that way after I made her feel so good.

"So…" she bites on her lip and meets my gaze. I have a suspicion of what she might ask and I think it's better for both of us if she doesn't.

I cut her off with one of my lame lines, "You know which day is on my calendar?"

She shakes her head a little, her long brown hair bounces off her breasts and I'm already getting hard again.

"Humpday." She giggles and I pull her body over mine drawing her in for a kiss. "Let me show you what we do on those days."

Her phone rings again, and she slips out of the bed and out of my arms. I miss her there instantly but I also like the view as she scrambles around looking for it. She finds it in her jacket pocket and looks up at me. "Thanks for the help."

I can't help the smirk on my face. "Sure thing," I wink.

Emily on all fours is something I might have to look at again later. *Later*? I bat the thought away. There is no later. I did what I said I was going to do. I gave her a new memory, the pleasure she deserved, and now we can both move on.

Her phone falls silent again. "I should really call him back." She says and slips into my t-shirt. It's like a too big dress for her, reaching almost to her knees and showing off her long neck and all of her right shoulder. It's sexy as hell.

"Do you know what you'll tell him?"

"The truth?"

I nod, "I could take you back, we can tell him together."

Her mouth falls slightly open and her eyes widen. Last time she looked at me like that we ended up here. Her lips are fucking mesmerising, swollen and bruised from my kisses, and I have an urge to kiss her again. I rip my eyes away and swing my legs off the bed. We should get going anyway.

"Shower." I point and mumble as she puts the phone to her ear and nods at me.

The hot water hits my skin like needles, it takes a second for my body to adjust to the heat. Planting my hands on the wall I dip my head under the spout letting the water run down over the back of my head, my neck, my back. I think about Emily wearing my shirt in the next room and my dick begins to swell and start to grow hard. "Fuck." I empty my lungs and try to empty my mind but I can't. She's every-where. She fills my head like I filled her pussy an hour ago, her sweet moans and rambled whimpers heat my blood, and fuck, I want her again. I'm walking through uncharted terri-tory and question every move I make. I brought her to my house, to my bed and held her after I fucked her. I don't hold women; I fuck them and leave. But I didn't want to let Emily go; I was loath to release her sweet little body that wriggled against mine. My blood heats and my body and brain battle one another. *This is stupid.* I turn off the hot water and all of my thoughts, focusing solely on getting myself clean, dressed and away from here. Away from her.

I finish off, dry, and get back into my room. Her gaze drifts along my naked torso where water droplets slide down to the towel wrapped around my hips. Her tongue darts out and she licks her lower lip and everything inside me tightens. No. This was a once-off thing. We both know it.

"Shower is all yours, I left you a clean towel." I go for casual. She needs to know we're done. I've done casual a million fucking times, so this should be easy. Except for some reason it's not.

Her face drops and her head tips a little as she stands and walks past me and out of the room. A second later I hear the click of the bathroom door before the pipes come alive. I stare at my door reminding myself why I can't go in there and instead get dressed.

———

I wait for her in the lounge. She's back in her oversized suit and her wet hair is slicked back, up in its bun. Everything is back where it belongs.

We get back into the car, the silence that we fell into back at the house follows us and sits between us like a passenger.

I clear my throat. "What did Daryl say?"

"He was pissed off."

My hand tightens around the steering wheel. I hate the way he treats her; guys like him need a good smacking to remind them of their place. "Look, I'll come inside with you and we'll tell—"

"No." Her hand on my thigh shuts me up and my eyes snap to it before returning to the road.

"Don't let him—"

"No. It's not what you think."

I suck in a calming breath before grinding out my question, "Ok. So why is he pissed off?"

"He needed me to organise an Uber for one of his "dates." One of the other guys helped him out."

I frown. "And Izabel?"

Her hands fist on her lap, "He forgot to tell me he had a courier pick it up. She was delivered to the house this morning."

"What about his 'With. Your. Life' bullshit?" She smiles at my imitation of Daryl, then shrugs.

"You'll have to ask him."

I nod and watch the road. A few hours ago, I was pissed off with the guy for sending me on this fool's errand, but after my afternoon with Emily, I'm happy to let it go—just this once.

1 2

Hunter

I nurse my aching head and exhale as my shift winds down. We're finally back at the house and Daryl has been giving me the run around all day. He doesn't seem to understand the concept of a bodyguard keeping him safe. He wanders off, vanishes and plays twisted, stupid games of hide and seek. I'm at my wits end with this guy. I'm too tired for his shit. I need some fresh air, but the air is hot and stifling. My shirt clings to my body with sweat and my jeans feel too tight. Fuck it, my own skin feels too tight. All I need is a cold shower, a cold beer and a good night's sleep.

I sign off, ending my shift and make a move towards my car. Except that I don't feel like going home and being alone there angry and frustrated. Instead, my legs just start walking back towards the house and the next thing I know I'm outside Emily's door, knocking.

She opens the door, her long hair bounces around her shoulders and she's wearing a sexy pyjama top that's cropped just above her belly, and tiny sleep shorts that barely cover her ass. "I don't know what I'm doing here," I say as my eyes keep drawing to that exposed sliver of skin.

I shouldn't be here; I should just turn away and leave but there's nowhere else I want to be. She steps aside wordlessly and lets me in. I fall onto her bed on my back and rub my palms into my eyes. "I don't know how you do it."

"Do what?"

"Put up with him."

"Sometimes you have to wade through a little bit of shit to get what you want."

"And what do you want?" My curiosity piques.

"I want you to get off my bed and go shower, you stink."

"Harsh." She's not wrong. Running around like a headless chicken in this humidity had me sweating all day. As I peel myself off her bed and walk over to her en-suit, I realised she never answered my question.

Showers are underrated. This one feels incredible. My hot angry skin relaxes and a sense of relief takes over me. I grab one of her bottles and notice it's a brand I know, it's expensive. Very expensive. I shower and dry myself off, eyeing everything else in the bathroom. Daryl must pay her very well. As I pat myself down I think about her sensible shoes and oversized suits - they're tailored and measured but have been made to make her look drab. A contradiction to the diamond earrings she wore at the gala, and that sexy as hell dress. Most PAs I know don't earn enough to afford an outfit like that. Then again, Daryl might be giving her some perks or maybe it was all rented. But then there were those lyrics she bid on.

I mull this over as I wrap the towel around my waist and grab my clothes not wanting to get back into them, then saunter back into the room. Emily is perched on her bed, legs crossed, leaning over her laptop. She looks up at me and red blooms on her cheeks. I like this effect on her much better than the usual sour faces I bring out in her.

I set my clothes aside and lay on her bed, hand tucked behind my damp hair as I study the screen. She's reading through a contract, her eyes focused, the tips of her fingers feathering over her lips. She's in her element.

"You never answered my question," I say

"Hmmm?" She turns to look at me and I know she wasn't listening at all "I'm almost done."

I nod and she turns back to the screen. I lay there in silence for a full second before my fingers find their way onto her knee and start a long slow journey upwards along her soft exposed skin. She slaps my hand away, never looking away from the screen.

Undeterred, my fingers brush over her thigh again, goosebumps explode on her skin and this garners me a long, irritated look. I smirk at Emily as she removes my hand for a second time and returns to her screen. She looks fucking beautiful when she pouts.

I can't help it now. I need a reaction. I want her full attention; she's certainly got mine. My knuckles find her skin again, and I run them along her thigh—god she feels good. Her head whips around and her eyes blaze.

"What are you doing?"

"Getting your attention," I smirk. Fuck she's stunning when she pretends she doesn't like me.

"I need to finish my work."

"Later." I run my hand back down to her knee and she shivers under my touch.

"Hunter, I need to do this."

"And I need you to answer my question." Her gaze slices to mine.

She sighs, her gaze leaves my face and rakes along my naked torso, "If I answer your question will you let me finish my work?"

I give her a two-finger salute, "Scout's honour." I finish with a smirk.

She rolls her eyes, "What question?"

My fingers tickle her thigh uninhibited, perfectly smooth skin that screams for me to take more. "Tell me what you want, Emily."

"Right now?"

"Yes."

"Right now I want you to shut up."

I'm about to protest when she straddles me in a swift move and her mouth finds mine, her tongue slips into my mouth and dances around, her hands creep up my neck plunging into my hair. My hands land on her hips and my fingers dig into those perfectly toned thighs. She gasps, breaking our kiss, "Hunter."

I love the way my name sounds on her lips, and I silence her with another kiss before she says anything else. Her hips begin to move gently against my hardening cock. Her mouth teases mine and her hips sink and rise till I groan with mounting frustration. I want more. I need more. I rip the shirt from her body and cup her breasts, rolling my thumbs over her nipples. She bites my lower lip in response and I hiss into her mouth.

Her mouth sinks to my neck, her teeth biting into my flesh dragging out against the skin. It's brutal, it's maddening. It's Emily.

She grips my towel and rips it open. My hard cock jerks between us as she tears away her tiny shorts and resumes her position. Her warm pussy sends me reeling as she glides over me, so wet and hot. My cock swells and strains, and I groan desperately wanting to be inside her.

"Emily," I groan and dig my fingers into her flesh. I've had enough of her games.

She kisses me again, a sly smile plays on her lips and her hungry eyes burn into mine. She grabs my cock, lines herself up, and ever so slowly sinks down onto me. I exhale almost in relief, except it's the opposite of what I feel. I'm feeling unhinged, watching her body move in a beautiful dance above mine, the way her breasts ripple between strands of long hair and her pouty mouth glistens.

I can't take it anymore. I wrap my arms around her and push up onto my knees, pressing her to my chest, my tongue flicks out and I catch her lips as I sink in deeper into her. She lets out a sweet, decadent sound that has my body tightening and my need more desperate. Her fingers rip into my shoulders as I dictate the pace, thrusting brutally into her.

Her thighs slap against mine, her breasts bounce with her movements and her head whips back. Fuck she is stunning, like a violent, beautiful earthquake. Everything shifts—her face, her body, her voice. Her breath comes out in hot sharp pants, and I'm so close.

My fingers dig into her as she pounds above me, her back arcs and her moans turn into desperate keening sounds that feed my own pleasure. My hips jerk up to meet her battering pace, and my greedy fingers glide up her stomach to roll over her nipples.

Her head snaps back and she cries out while quivering above me. Hands clutch my back and she grinds me into her with a jarring pulsing climax. Her tight pussy clenches around me and I explode with a shattering orgasm, convulsing violently with her as she drags me deeper still.

We stay there for a few moments, catching our breaths, my head nestled in the crook of her neck, her tousled hair tickling my face. I find her lips and kiss her, finding my breath, enjoying the feel of her soft lips on mine. I weave my hands through the loose strands and gather her hair deepening the kiss. Fuck. I love the way she tastes and the way that her lips and body feel against me. I break the kiss on that thought. It's not a good one to have, not when all I needed was to wind down. I'm not looking for anything else.

Emily smiles at me. She's stunning all wild and sweet, with her post-sex hair and sweaty sheen making her body glow. *Shit*.

She gets off me and I collapse onto the bed, stretching my burning muscles. She lays down beside me, her head on my chest. My hand automatically wraps around her even though I know I should get dressed and leave. Instead, my fingers travel along her naked back and her hot breath tickles my chest while her fingers draw lines between my abs. Like we're mapping one another, learning one another—and it needs to stop. But maybe later. Cause right now, this feels too good, and I'm too tired to go anywhere.

13

Hunter

I wake up before the alarm with Emily in my arms. It's new and has been happening more often than not over the past week. Every time my shift ends I consider going home. But no matter how hard I try my legs carry me to her door, into her arms, to the soft feel of her skin and the delicious taste of her body. I'm insatiable.

I shift a little and she murmurs in her sleep, sliding away from me. I tighten my grip, keeping her close. She nuzzles into my chest and I catch the scent of her hair, some tropical combination, but not overly sweet—subtle and delicate, like her. It's easy to lie here in the quietness. Listening to her breathe, feeling her warmth against me, and telling myself that this is the most convenient arrangement I've ever had. I don't have to stand outside some door and go to a smelly fucking cubicle to have my cock sucked. No, Emily is a master at that and last night she introduced me to a new art form. My cock hardens thinking about her mouth wrapped around me, her pouty lips as they swallowed up my shaft and drew back slowly, teasing me mercilessly. I bite my lower lip to keep from groaning as images of Emily compound with the feel of her in my arms.

She must feel my body stiffen and shift as she moans a little before opening her eyes. The hair is stuck to her face and small wrinkles of sleep gather around her puffy, sleepy eyes. Her brow gathers in a slight frown and she moans, "It's still early."

"Go back to sleep," I whisper but she rolls away from me and stretches. Slender arms over her head as her back arches and a purr spills from her lips. Fuck she's beautiful.

"Who can sleep with you tossing and turning non-stop?"

I draw her back to me, wanting to feel her skin against mine, "Not my fault, you make it so *hard* for me to stay still"

She tries to slap me away, feeling my erection against the soft curve of her ass. "Hunter." She moans my name, trying to sound grumpy but utterly failing.

"Mm-hmm?" I murmur against her neck, laying a kiss on her soft skin.

"Go away." She pretends and rolls towards me.

"Make me," I whisper to her before kissing her. It's a soft gentle touch of our lips that has my body burning. I flip her onto her back and settle between her legs, I'm already light-headed and drunk on the delicate scent of her skin.

I slide inside her easily, her warmth enveloping me instantly and I sigh, almost relieved. Catching her lips with mine, I move in her, calm strokes. I want her with me. Her caramel eyes locked on mine, the thrill of it thrums from my body.

I'm slow, taking my time with her. I want her writhing in pleasure. I want to be the man she sees in me. the one I'm not even sure is in there.

She claws at my back saying my name in a long, slow exhale and a shiver wracks through my body as her hips roll to meet mine, making desire run deep into my veins. She's so fucking beautiful when she wants me.

I drag my cheek against hers, my whiskers rasping against her smooth skin, and line up our faces, the way she is looking at me is anything but cold, but as soon as I see that flash of heat her head rolls back and her body arches towards me lengthening the graceful curves of her neck accentuating the hollows above her collarbones begging my teeth to sink into her flesh. And they do, grazing the skin, tasting her.

I speed up, my breaths quicken and I pull her closer to me, I need to be deeper inside her. The hunger in her breath turns my need from primitive to dangerous, from gentle to savage. I mould her into me as I pound into her, swallowing her moans, fucking her hard, owning her, making her mine, watching her body light up for me. Her orgasm comes hard and brutal. She clenches against me, digging into my back, calling out my name, dragging my pleasure till I cum hard inside her, riding her waves of pleasure.

I collapse into her heaving chest and kiss the spot between her breasts before I roll away from her. If I'm not careful I could get used to this—to her waking up tangled in my arms and saturating me with her sweet smells and intoxicating body. She lifts up on an elbow and kisses me before her face breaks into a smile. Sliding out of the bed, she saunters into the bathroom with her rounded ass on display. A minute later the taps come to life in her en-suite, and I remind myself that I'm only here because it's convenient, that having Emily in my arms is just a way to release all my tension after working with her boss all day. I then remind myself that she's naked in the shower, and I throw the blanket off me and I go join her.

It's a rare day off that I plan to enjoy in full, right after I finish taking care of some crucial life admin. Having stayed with Emily the last week meant I had a pile of washing to get through, layers of dust to contend with, and a fridge emptier than Wolf's head. But as I think about the chores waiting for me at home, Emily's ass snuggles against me and erases any other thoughts.

I kiss her neck and she murmurs a sleepy good morning. I love the way she takes forever to wake up—fighting sleep, snatching every last fragment of her dreams before she forces her eyes open to face another day.

I should get going, but I don't want to leave this bed. Instead, I snake my arms around her and pull her closer to me.

She snuggles back into me, her body doing dangerous things to mine. "Didn't you say something about needing to get things done today?"

"Mm-hmm." Suddenly, the only thing I want to do today is her.

"Then shouldn't you get going?" She purrs against me as my hand slithers up her torso and finds her breasts.

"Are you trying to get rid of me?" I whisper into her ear before laying a kiss on her shoulder.

She half turns towards me and throws me a sexy smile, "You can stay, for now."

"For now?" I pinch her nipple, making her scream and jump in my arms half surprised, half delighted.

"Hunter!" She giggles and squirms in my arms, and I can't get enough of that sound, of the feel of her against me. She turns to me and studies my face as if she is mulling something over, "Do you want to do something today, like go out and see a show or something?"

"Don't you have to work?"

"Daryl can manage a day without me."

"Can he though?"

She giggles and the sound makes every bit of me come alive. I put it down to the massive erection I'm sporting. "He'll be fine." She kisses me gently before dragging my lower lip between her teeth.

"Yeah, guess he'll just have to be," I growl as I wrap myself in Emily.

We get out at Marble Arch station and make our way towards the park. Emily takes a minute to admire the Arch, the splendidly carved stonework, while I take the time to admire her. She's the real work of art.

She smiles at me before slipping her hand into mine. I say nothing. The sensation is foreign and unfamiliar and she shouldn't get used to it. But I allow it. This one time.

"It's beautiful around here," she says as she keeps looking around.

"You don't come here often?"

"Between Daryl and his tours and studio visits, I rarely get time to do much of anything."

"And when you do?"

She shrugs, "I've never really liked London very much."

"Why?"

She looks away at the path ahead and keeps the answer to herself. I let it go, for now. She spots an ice cream van and makes her way towards it. She's like an excited kid as she reads over the limited menu.

"What can I get you, miss?" An over-enthusiastic kid leans out of the window and ogles her.

She gives him a stunning smile and asks for a strawberry vanilla soft serve. He beams at her till I clear my throat and step a little closer. His smile vanishes. Finally, someone other than Emily who I have that effect on.

"And for you, sir?"

I tighten my grip on Emily's hand. "Do you have any salted caramel?"

She turns to me with question marks in her eyes, "I didn't take you for a salted caramel kind of guy."

I shrug, "It's a new flavour I've been trying out."

She beams at me before taking her cone from the now sulking kid. I pay for our ice cream before smirking at him and turning away.

It's hard not to stare at Emily licking her soft serve. Her tongue leaves long deep furrows in the whipped desert as the two flavours slowly melt into one.

I rip my eyes away and concentrate on my own cone as we walk along in silence for a while.

When we find ourselves near the water I find a bench and sit, she follows me and tucks herself close. I'm not sure why I don't move away.

"You know your way around here." It's a statement that sounds like a question. So I give her what she wants.

"We used to come here all the time in summer when we were kids."

"We?"

"Me, Red, and Wolf. We used to walk along the Serpentine and eat ice cream and help ourselves to a few unattended purses."

Her head lifts to mine, her mouth slightly open and her eyes large.

"What? We were kids, we were hungry, and we wanted ice cream." I wink at her and she relaxes again as I nudge my large frame into her much smaller one.

"Sounds like you guys had a lot of fun."

"We did. I wanted to give Red a childhood that was more than waiting for me at home alone while I worked, and a half-filled belly."

"It sounds like you did a great job."

I shrug. "What were you like as a kid?"

"I was happy sometimes."

"Sometimes?"

She bites into her cone and a drop of ice cream coats the rim of her lips. Without thinking I lift my hand to her mouth and wipe it away. My thumb brushes over her lower lip and drags it slowly. Her eyes latch onto mine and I lift her chin before my lips brush hers and my tongue swipes away at the remnants of the flavour left by her desert. The kiss is gentle, full of tenderness, intoxicating and all wrong. I pull away and try to regain myself.

I clear my throat wondering what the hell that was, before turning back to the water. "What does sometimes mean?"

"What?" She blinks at me a few times as if seeing me for the first time that day.

"You said you were happy *sometimes*."

Her smile drops a little and she scoops the rest of the ice cream into her mouth. "No one is happy all the time."

She's diverting again but this time I don't want to let it go. "Emily." My voice is firm enough to let her know what I'm asking.

She sighs and her mouth twists a little. "I was happy with my mom. She was my best friend, for a long time my only friend. As I said, my dad wasn't around. His idea of parenting was to send presents and money and not to be present at all."

She draws in a small breath before continuing, "My mom always stood up for him and said it was his work that kept him away. But at night, I'd sometimes hear them talk and her cry and beg him to come back, and how everything was already broken so why bother hiding it. I didn't really know what any of it meant, not till much later when it was too late anyway."

"What happened to being tragically in love?"

"That was their tragedy; she was utterly, devastatingly

and tragically in love with him but he loved her from afar, putting his career and friendship before us. By the time he realised that we should have been his priority all along she was gone."

"How?"

Her beautiful eyes swell with tears and I feel her pain, it's palpable and raw. "Drunk driver. Wrong place at the wrong time. Her head injuries were too devastating, and she never recovered."

She wipes the unshed tears from her eyes and I pull her into me, wanting to shelter her from all that pain, knowing I never can.

"Is that why you don't like it here?"

She shrugs against me, "Too much pain in such a big city, I can't seem to get away from it anywhere."

"Pain always clings to us harder than happiness. It colours our world in darker hues and shades. It teaches us more, even lessons we're not ready to learn." It's a harsh truth I'd had to learn.

We sit in silence for a short while taking in the sunshine and the world around us before I stand up and lead us through the park.

"How long have you been singing?" I break our silence as we near the edge of the park.

"All my life."

"So, what's the real reason you haven't pursued it?"

"I have."

"Sure," I say and hate the way it sounds coming out of my mouth.

She pouts for a second before she starts speaking, "Bearing your soul on stage makes you very vulnerable. It's the kind of nakedness you share with the world. Maybe I just haven't been ready."

"And now?"

"I don't know. I guess there's never an ideal time for

anything. But if I don't try now, if I don't chase what I want, I'll let it slip through my fingers and live with that regret."

I nod. Regret is like a snow globe—a whole other moment in time caught forever inside a bubble. You can shake it up and look at it from every angle you want, but in the end, the flakes just settle back into place and nothing has changed. It sits on a shelf, gathering dust and reminds you of what could have been.

14

Emily

Tonight is the night.

I look in the mirror and promise myself - just like I've been promising myself every day for the last few days. I'm going to tell him. Hunter has been coming into my room night after night and since our outing to Hyde Park, our days have been spent trading smiles and hidden glances. His long, languishing kisses and hot body make me burn before I fall asleep in his strong arms. But I need to know if this is heading anywhere and what he wants, especially after this morning. I'm still breathless thinking about it.

The kitchen is empty and I find myself flicking looks over to the doorway looking for his shadow knowing it won't be there. Despite our nights together and whispered conversations I've stood my ground. He can get in my pants but not in the house, not during his shifts anyway.

The day feels longer than usual. Despite our late departure and Daryl's session in the studio, through all my phone calls to venues and ticket agencies, the clock doesn't want to move. Time stretches like a water drop on the end of a tap.

I can't help but steal looks at Hunter. The way his t-shirt strains with every movement of his biceps, his messy blonde hair, his razor-sharp jaw, ghosted smiles and silly poses he throws my way every time he catches me out. They make my heart stampede in my chest and run through the rest of my body.

When we finally arrive back at the house, I can barely digest my dinner and make a hasty return to my room. My heart skitters and my stomach coils with a thousand unspoken words that need to burst out of me. I draw in a long breath and snatch another look at my clock. His shift will be over soon.

The heat stifles me, and the walls threaten to close in. No matter what I do, I can't shake this feeling. Like being hooked up to an electric fence set to low voltage, I know it won't kill me but it's uncomfortable as hell. I need to get out of my head and out of this room.

The knock startles me even though I'm expecting it, making my heart rate surge. I open the door and it stops beating completely when I find him there. Like every other night he's shown up at my door, he's there leaning on the door frame a sly smile across his face, his eyes sparkle.

"Fancy meeting you here," he says in his playful tone.

"It's you who seem to keep showing up?"

"What can I say, I have to check the place out, you know, security stuff? And this room happened to have the sweetest piece of ass in it." My heart cramps. *Just my ass?*

"It's not the only thing sweet about me." I shake it off and smirk.

"Oh yes, baby, I know." He pushes the door open and kisses me hard before pulling away and studying my face.

I graze his bruised lips with mine and a smile spreads across his beautiful face. A face to fall in love with, *and I have.*

Hard and deep and inexplicably so. My heart skitters as I brush my fingers across his jaw, letting the bristles rasp against my fingers and take a steeling breath. My whole body shakes, as fear tries to grip me, "I wanted to ask you something."

"Mm-hmm," he purrs as those hot lips brush my neck and he pushes me onto the bed flipping us over so that he can grind my hips into his.

"What's this thing between us?"

"My cock?" His eyebrows wiggle and a brash smile spreads across his face.

I chew on my lip and try again, "No Hunter. What are we doing?"

His body stiffens for a second and his mouth leaves my body. "Why does it matter? Why do we have to define it?"

"I just…" my heart pounds against my rib cage, my pulse surges.

His lips find my neck again and he grazes my skin with his teeth, "We're having fun, don't spoil it by turning it into something it's not." My heart twists and sinks as he kisses lower down. "I'm just here for you until the real thing comes along."

"The real thing?" My eyes burn with tears.

His lips trace my collar bone, "That thing other people call love."

My heart lurches, wrecking my hollowing chest and I suck in a deep breath wiping away my unshed tears. "You still don't believe in love?"

He kisses my chest, "Just something people like you say."

"People like me?"

"Romantics, poets—desperate, empty people who think that word will fill them with something that isn't really there."

"And trap you?" I finish for him and feel him smile against my skin before he purrs a yes and wraps his hot mouth around my nipple. My body reacts even as it falls apart on the inside.

"But love exists." I persist, though I don't know why.

"Fleetingly." His tongue flicks my nipple.

I sink my hands into his hair. I want his attention, but he's focused elsewhere and I don't want to lose my train of thought. "It has to exist."

"Why? Why are you so certain it exists? Why does it have to be more than a few chemicals in the brain playing tricks?"

"Wow." I push his head away, and at last he looks at me, confusion marring his face.

"Is the truth too harsh?"

"You just don't have to—"

"What? State facts?"

"Love is more than just chemicals."

"Love is lust in disguise. It's just two people wanting to get in each other's pants until that feeling is over and then they find their next 'love interest'."

"People are more than skin deep. Of course, there is an initial attraction that's physical, but people have other endearing qualities that make them beautiful. That makes you want to stay and spend time with them. Endlessly."

"Or the guy just knows it's a sure thing and he can get what he wants."

"Wow." I move a little farther away from him.

"Where is all this coming from?" He leans on his elbow, his half-naked body on display and I take it all in, wondering if it's the last time I'll ever see it.

"So, you don't believe people can fall in love forever? That the children they have together and the life they build is anything more than a phase? A chemical imbalance that lasts too long?"

"It's all a concept designed to trap us into something unnatural."

"So, love and children are just traps?"

He falls onto his back, the hard on he had moments ago shrinking, and he runs his hands over his face. "I'm not sure what you want me to say, Emily, you knew how I feel about all this. We've talked about this before."

I nod.

Something changes in his face, and his eyes darken, "The fact is, that not everyone stays. Not if they feel trapped, forced into something they don't want to be a part of. Children don't always keep people together. It's not fair on the children who get abandoned." His tone strikes a chord in my heart.

"Just because it happened to you—"

"Don't," he hisses.

"Is that why you're so angry? Is that why you think love doesn't exist?"

"I don't want to talk about that right now. You know how I feel. My parents should have never had us. They were obviously more "in love" with the idea of the notion than actually wanting it. Love is a made-up concept to disguise the fact that two people want each other, and when they grow old and bitter, they wonder why they stayed." He lifts me up and rolls away, his eyes shimmering in the dim lights, "Look at your own family."

I purse my lips and tears prickle my eyes.

"Emily, I'm sorry. I didn't mean that last bit. What's this really about?" His voice softens as he looks at me intently.

My body knots and strangles like a constrictor is wrapping itself around me and squeezing out all my bravery. It's pointless. I shake my head, "Nothing, let's just get some sleep."

He huffs as he rolls onto his side facing away from me, and my heart shatters inside me.

Did I really think he would change, for me? I keep waiting for him to roll back over, to face me, to erase all his harsh words. But he doesn't. He lays there motionless, but I can tell he isn't asleep. His body is stiff and rigid. He obviously didn't come here to sleep.

⸻

I listen to his breathing. His body tangled with mine feels perfect, and yet, I know what I need to do.

As soon as I detach myself from him, my chest squeezes like my heart forgets how to beat and the heat evaporates off my skin.

But I have to leave, I have to go. He thinks of himself as a placemat for the real thing, unaware that for me, he could have been. A shiver wracks through my body and everything hurts. He never saw how much I love him, how much I want him, how much he means to me; but then again, he never wanted me in the way I wanted him, never so fierce and hungry—I was convenient, I was here, he didn't have to go far to find what he wanted. While here I was, dying on the inside knowing he could have been the one to hold my heart forever. Though I have no right feeling any of this.

I get dressed silently, my stomach turning in revolt. I ignore the ache in my chest, the way my heart feels like it's getting hacked at with a machete. I grab my bag, stuffing it with a few necessities. I'll have everything I need when I go home. *Home*—not *my* home.

I sigh as I walk toward the door. I feel like a boat stranded in the middle of a big tumultuous sea pulling the anchor up and drifting away from safety, from Hunter. But then again, maybe he is the storm that's going to wreck me.

Maybe he already has.

Maybe he was right all along—pain is so much purer, more vicious, and forceful than our happiness ever was. With an angry wave and scathing words, he's washed it all away.

But I'm not going to whimper and cry and break, not in front of him. Later in the safety of the dark, where I can dissolve into the shadows. Now I'm going to get up and do what has to be done.

Hunter

I wake up to insistent buzzing and a cold bed. I search around for Emily's body that's usually curled up against me, only to find empty space. I reach over to the bedstand and find the buzzing. My phone.

I bolt up. Shit. It's well after nine. Why the hell didn't Emily wake me up?

"Hello?" My voice cracks into the phone.

"Where are you, man? It's after nine." James the night shift guy sounds pissed.

"Yeah. I'll be there in ten." I hang up and rush from the bed and into the en-suite. I throw some water over my face and go for my morning piss. I'm shaking off when I see it, and everything inside me seizes.

No.

I tuck myself into my boxers and reach over grabbing the box. *First Response Pregnancy Test*. What the fuck? Surely not? I was careful. *We* were careful. Weren't we? I feel the blood drain from my face as I open the bin and search. I find the test and glare at the pink plus sign in the middle of the plastic stick.

My knees wobble.

No.

She's pregnant?

Is that what last night was all about?

"Fuck" I swear at the room and plunge my fingers into my hair, digging my hands into my scalp as they rake through.

The next few minutes go by as if I'm in slow motion. A slew of thoughts smash through me.

Is she ok? What does she want to do? Does she want to keep it? Do I? Am I ready for this? Are we?

I am buried under an avalanche of paranoia. I don't want to be a dad—not now, maybe not ever. My lifestyle isn't conducive to a family, and then there's Red.

"Shit." I grab my phone and dial Emily's number as I slam my feet into my jeans and hop into them. The phone goes to voicemail.

I try again, throwing my t-shirt over my head and brushing my hair out of my face with my fingers. No answer.

I run downstairs and out of the house, signing in and relieving James from his shift. He's not happy and I don't give a shit. I feel as though I am in a hurricane. My whole world is tilted and blown over and I need to talk to Emily.

The day drags on, and there is no sign of her. She doesn't join us at the studio and doesn't pick up any of my calls. I've already left her over twenty messages. By the end of the day, I feel like I've been run over by a train. Anger, confusion, and frustration all rage inside me, each stabbing and twisting my insides. I sign off and knock on Emily's door. There's no answer. After a second knock, I try the door handle, the door cracks open.

"Emily?" I'm greeted with silence, and I step into the dark room. I flick the light on and find the room exactly how I had left it that morning. She hasn't been back. I decide to wait. I sit on the edge of the bed just to stand up again and pace like a caged animal. Where the hell is she? I try her number for the hundredth time and throw my phone across the room when the automated voice tells me I've reached her voice mail. "Fuck," I roar and my fist hits her wall, leaving behind a large cavity and a trail of blood on my knuckles.

The next few hours feel like a torture device designed to send me over the abyss. My jaw hurts from the endless grinding and everything feels tight, especially my chest. I feel so many things I don't even know where to begin, or how to process this—my body aches.

I rub my palms into my eyes, thinking for the hundredth time about my words last night. How I pushed her away, how I made sure we both agreed and knew it was nothing more than two bodies needing relief at the end of each day working for an intolerable fool. It would have never lasted, never worked between us. It was all circumstantial and fleeting. I would have gone on to another job in a few days, and she would have gone on tour with Daryl and our paths would never cross again. Except that the more I feed myself the idea, the more I hate the fact that I could be wrong, that we could have been more. And now, she could be pregnant with my child. Mine. Ours. Do I even want that? Do I get a say? Could I even make that work? Could we be a family?

Questions swirl and crash inside my skull like a crazed, out of control pinball machine till I fall into a fitful sleep.

Her warm legs snake through mine and all I feel is her naked heat against my body. I don't remember hearing her come in or when I got naked, but I don't care. She's here and she's mine. I grab her hips and flip her on her back, I'm inside her in a second and she's hot and wet and willing. Her moans are so fucking sweet, I never want to leave this bed. I don't want to break our kiss or pull out of her, I want to make her quiver and sweat and come. Forever.

My eyes pop open, and I blink in the dark room. I'm fully dressed on her bed, and I'm all alone.

"Shit" I run my hands along my face and draw in a long breath. I reach for my phone. Nothing.

I ignore my massive hard on, shower and dress for the

day. I call her. An automated voice tells me the number I've dialled no longer exists.

———

I go through another day and my insides are a playground of emotion, swinging from anger to frustration to wonder and sheer, white panic. I try her number a few more times just to get the same message. The number doesn't exist. When I ask Daryl about Emily he frowns then says she just quit—up and left—and left him in the fucking shit. I ruin his mood for the rest of the day and pay for it. As if I wasn't suffering enough.

I don't bother going to her room when I finish my shift, she won't be there. Instead, I go to the office. I need to pull a few favours and find out where Emily is.

15

Hunter

I sit in my car and watch the windows. It's pathetic really. It's my bloody office and I should be able to just walk in there and do what I want. But there are already too many rumours and too many smirks, and I'm sick of everyone's shit. I just need to be alone.

The lights go off and I watch Rob swagger out of the office, phone to his ear, smile on his face. Probably organising his date for the night. He gets into his BMW and checks himself out in the mirror before backing up and taking off down the street. When his lights vanish, I get out of my car, cross the road, and let myself into the office.

It smells like some kind of curry, and I feel sorry for whoever is going to be spending any time with Rob tonight. I smirk, fuck him, fuck them both. I'm not in a generous mood. I turn on the computer and fall into my chair while the screen comes alive.

I find Daryl's employee file and pull out Emily's clearance paperwork.

Emily Shepard, twenty-five, born in West London. I quirk my eye at this. She didn't seem the type. Then again, I have a feeling apart from knowing her body intimately, I know very little else about little miss Shepard. However, I'm about to get very well acquainted. The file isn't very detailed and should have been flagged to Rob as suspicious information.

I take note of the address listed in her paperwork, scribble it down and shove the paper into my pocket before I start to dig in. I open up one of my fake Facebook accounts and input Emily Shepard. There are less than ten profiles under that name. None of them appear to be hers. I use some open source tools online to go through all the other usual social media apps. She doesn't exist online, not even a LinkedIn profile. She was talking about making contacts and getting to know people so this strikes me as odd. I search for her parents, all the information about them is vague at best or conveniently unavailable. There is no home address associated with them. When I look into her university qualifications there is a graduate called Emily Shepard, she did graduate top of her class, but she is dark-haired with slanted, piercing blue eyes and her face is round and chubby. None of this makes any bloody sense.

A Google search yields no results. The name is ordinary and common. I pull out a list of local hospitals and start calling each one searching for an Emily Shepard. I'm both relieved and annoyed when three hours later I still haven't found her.

I look at the clock. It's too late to call Mark at the cop shop, his shift would have ended a few hours ago. I kick myself for waiting this long. But even if I did, I might be well out of favours with him. Still, I can always owe him one. With his access, he can run her name through his database and search her credit card numbers.

I shake my head feeling like a stalker. How far am I willing to take this?

I slam the door to my car; frustration skitters along my neck. My search has yielded nothing. I push the car into gear and hurtle out of my parking space and onto the road. I drive too fast and too recklessly, but I feel reckless. Anger sweeps over me. She can't just do this, she can't just crash into my life, make me feel this way, and then fall out of it without a word.

I find a parking spot down the road from her apartment and jog down to her place. I watch from across the road feeling like a creep. The place is dark, with no movement. I keep watching just in case. Telling myself it's part of the job to use counter-surveillance techniques. When after a while nothing changes, I go to knock on the door. Lightly at first. When no one answers I pound louder. "Emily? Emily!"

A door opens, but it's not hers. It's the neighbour. An older woman that might be in her late sixty's. She eyes me suspiciously and steps back into the safety of her own home, holding the door firmly, ready to slam it shut. I can't blame her really, a guy my size pounding on the door after midnight. Shit, I didn't realise how late it was. We stare at each other for a few seconds before I try for a smile.

"Hi, I'm looking for Emily, is she here? Has she been here?"

The woman's eyes narrow slightly, the suspicion etched deep into her face. "You mean Emilia?"

Emilia.

"Yeah, has she been in?"

"Not for months, she often travels with her boss and doesn't spend much time here. I have her key to look after Murry."

"Murry?" I grind my teeth as I wonder how I will deal with this Murry.

"Her plant."

I bite down a grin. Typical Emily naming her fucking plants. And still another thing I knew nothing about. "And has she been in this week?"

"Who are you?"

"A friend." I try to erase the tension from my face and smile again.

"A friend would have her phone number." The gap in her door shrinks.

"Wait. Please." I take a tiny step forwards not wanting to scare her. "We were working together and she just took off, I just want to know if she's ok."

The woman's face softness a little and she sighs. "I didn't see her, but when I went in this morning a few things had been moved around and removed."

"A few things?"

"Her wardrobe is empty and she took Murry."

My head drops in defeat. My last lead is gone just like Emily. I turn to leave then swivel back around, "Hey, just one last thing. Why do you call her Emilia?"

"Cause that's her name." The woman closes her door, and I know our conversation is over.

I get back to my car, pull out my phone and type in Emilia Shepard. Hundreds of images pop up. I scroll through a few then throw my phone on the passenger seat and smash my palms on my steering wheel. "Fuck." My growl echoes in my car.

I'm missing something and I don't know what it is. It's late and I'm tired, so I give up for the night and go home. I walk into my empty house to find all my discarded laundry still waiting and a layer of dust mocking me. I know the fridge will be empty too, but that's tomorrow's problem. I crash onto my bed and fall into a restless sleep.

The rest of the week is no better. Despite my efforts, I

can't locate Emily—if that's even her name. Mark refuses to use his police resources to help dig into her. It's bullshit, but he keeps going on about privacy laws and I don't want to hear it. Daryl is an agitated mess and I'm babysitting a beehive with some angry fucking bees. I go home stung, bitter and irate, and even if I don't want to admit it, I miss her.

<hr>

Tom pulls up at the airport and goes to deal with Daryl's bags. The rock star shuffles out of his car, two women climb out behind him, both giggling and ogling the private jet. He sends them to the stairs with a cliche smack on the bum and watches as they walk away. Apparently, he doesn't like to fly alone.

"Well, thanks mate." He looks at me and offers his hand which I shake.

"Thank you, sir." We've already had the 'if you're ever back in town' talk. Of course, I didn't mean it, but it's expected.

"You're a free agent now."

"Yes, sir." I nod and wait for him to leave. He doesn't, instead, he watched the two women climb up the stairs, their short skirts riding up their exposed thighs.

"Free to go where you want and do what you need to do."

I nod again wondering what the fuck he wants.

"They're a thing of beauty, hey lad?" He waves at the two women who stand atop the stairs and wait for him.

"Sure." The heat beats down my face and all I want is to get out of there and forget about Daryl Dark. And Emily.

"You know, when there's something that beautiful waiting for you, that makes your heart come alive, you should chase it."

He looks at me meaningfully, like he thinks I know what

he means. He nods, smirks, and pushes away from the car. "Don't live on memories, they're never as good as the real thing." He walks away, leaving me with his strange bit of wisdom then rushes up the stairs where he swoops on his two companions, they giggle before disappearing inside the jet.

16

Hunter

I reach over to the bedstand and check my phone. No calls from Emily.

It's been two months. I haven't heard from her. She's clearly moved on.

I don't remember the last time I had a day off. My body is a wreck and Wolf insisted. Something about days of stubble on my jaw and dark circles under my eyes. He's right. I've been working nonstop for weeks, living on coffee and a few hours of sleep each night. The work keeps me occupied and the loud music quiets my mind. The occasional blow job from some random girl helps, but not as much as I'd hoped. I've been so fucking grumpy lately; nothing is as much fun as it used to be.

I've tried to move on. Screwed a few girls—happy to make them smile. But fuck it, I leave their bed emptier than when I walked in. Everyone else just feels average compared to her, and there's the nagging feeling that shadows me wherever I go. Could she be carrying my child?

Ever since Emily vanished it's like being thirsty in the rain. My throat feels dry and my lips cracked, and no matter how much I drink, the thirst won't be quenched. A never-ending drought I can't break.

My dreams of her are so vivid, I wake up hard and in pain. My hands grip the sheets, missing the shape of her ass. She consumes my thoughts, drives my emotions, and I find myself spending too much of my free time searching for her. It's easy to tell myself that all I feel is curiosity, the need to know where she is, how she is, and if she's carrying a part of me inside her.

The idea of an imaginary baby is hard to grasp, and every time I think of her having our child and keeping it from me, my blood boils under my skin. I know what abandonment feels like, what it's like to know you're not loved or wanted. No one deserves that. The thoughts gnaw at me endlessly like a ravenous monster and everything around me suffers.

My ringtone pierces the quiet room and my heart leaps. It's a ringtone I haven't heard for a long time.

"Hey." My voice croaks down the phone.

"Hey. How are you doing?"

"Fine." I lie.

"Shaw seems to disagree." Red dismisses my words.

"Tell Wolf he should mind his own business and go fuck himself."

"How about you come have coffee with me instead? We have some things to talk about."

"Yeah, I'd like that." I would. I miss Red too. Why are all the women in my life angry at me?

"Great, come around at two."

She hangs up and I let the phone drop onto the bed. Maybe we can resolve some of our shit and move on.

The door opens and Red's face draws into a frown, "You look like shit."

"Nice to see you, too." I give her a tired smile before she wraps herself around me. I gather her to me, giving her a long hug. I think we both need it.

I release her and she steps aside letting me in. The place radiates happiness and it makes me feel a little ill. I follow her into the lounge and she gestures for me to sit down. I sink into the comfortable sofa and look at my sister. She looks good. That son of a bitch is actually keeping his promise and I feel like a right twat. She could have felt like this for much longer.

She goes into the kitchen and comes back with two steaming cups in her hands.

"You look happy," I tell her as she hands me my coffee.

"I am." She grins.

"Stop! I don't want to know."

Her grin widens and I push all the thoughts out of my head, vacating my brain and concentrating solely on the coffee in my hands. I sip, then meet my sister's scrutinising eyes. "How have you been?"

Her eyes dart around the room then meet mine again. "Really good actually. I've got another show coming up in a few months, and Becca says this is the one that will set me up."

Her eyes light up and she's all animated as she speaks, her whole body joins in the conversation, limbs flying around as her mouth moves. "I'm so proud of you, Red."

"Thanks." Her smile rips through her face.

"Look, Red, I'm sorry—"

"Don't." She holds up her hand and I fall silent. "I know your intentions were coming from a good place. Everything you ever did for me, you did because you cared. You had no choice, you had to be strong. You've always been strong."

I scoff. Everyone keeps telling me that—*you'll be ok, you're strong*. All they ever see is a boulder, a solid rock that can take every hit. Every lash of the elements, the scorching sun, the whipping winds, the raging seas of everyone's fucking emotions. But boulders get scuffed, and over time, they shrink to rocks, and then pebbles. Sure on the outside they'll always be solid and strong, they'll always look like a rock, but no one will ever notice how much of themselves they've shed, how much they lose over time as they erode, how much pain and hurt and anguish they go through.

Her voice pulls me away from my thoughts. "Let's just move on. I think we've both said everything we're ever going to need to say about it. I needed time to process it and I took it. Shaw helped me see your point of view too." She sighs, "Let's just chalk all that to the past. I'm happy, I'm safe, and I'm not angry. Not anymore."

I nod. I guess there's nothing left to say then.

"Now, what's going on with you? Why are you walking around like someone killed your cat?"

"What cat?"

"Hunter." She folds her hands across her chest and stares me down.

I put my cup down and run my hands over my thighs a few times before I lean back and look at the ceiling. "There's this… person."

"Emily?" My eyes snap to hers and she shrugs, "Everyone knows."

My brow arches so high it feels like it touches my hairline.

"Come on. You're grumpy, you take your shit out on everyone at work, you're working inhuman hours, and Shaw said something about your code 22 average dipping to non-existent."

I'm going to kill that fucker. I shake my head. "Well, then you know."

"Did you tell her how you feel?"

"What are you talking about?"

"That you love her."

"I don't—"

"Hunter." She slices through my words.

"Red." I taunt.

"Just admit it."

I sigh. I never told her, but maybe it's because until this very minute I wasn't even sure that this is what this is. Fuck.

"No, I didn't tell her," I blow out a breath, "not that it matters. I blew it. I thought I'd be happier if I just let it run its course and end."

"Happier or safer?"

"Isn't that the same thing?"

Red looks at me, her eyes locked on mine, "I know you had it hardest. I know that everyone left you—mom, dad, me..." Her mouth twists a little, "But you've missed out on enough, given up enough. You've always had to be the one that's reliable and strong, a permanent fixture that fixes everything for everyone. It's your turn. Stop hiding, stop thinking that you are not worth being loved, of holding someone's attention so completely that you're the centre of their world."

"Red—"

"No. It's not too late. You've kept yourself *safe* for too long, now you need to be happy. Why do you need a safety net if you're never going to take a risk?"

"Red—"

"If you don't tell her, then one day someone else will."

The thought of another man touching Emily, instantly steels my armour. "I think she may be pregnant."

Red's eyes light up and the tightening around her eyes fills the silent room like a speech. "You're not sure?"

"I might have said something awful before she up and left…"

Red squared her back and glares at me, "What the fuck did you say, Hunter?"

"I might have said something along the lines of kids are a trap…" I don't get to finish my sentence. Red stands up and her hand swings towards my head. I catch it before it connects and she snatches it away burning me with an irate look.

"What the hell is wrong with you?"

"I didn't know…"

"It's not the point!"

"I know. I know! I stuffed up, she's gone, and I fucking miss her. It's eating me up."

Red smiles at me, and her face beams again, "Good. Now go get her."

I rake my fingers through my hair dragging them along my scalp. "I can't, she's gone."

"Find her."

"You think I haven't been looking? I can't find her."

"Look harder."

I nod and sink into the couch, defeat weighing heavily on my shoulders. Red slides next to me, a hug from her would make me feel better. But before I can react, she swings at me again and hits me around the head. I guess I better look harder.

***

I hang around for a while longer, Red shows me pictures of her time away with Wolf and talks about her artwork. I want to be more interested but my mind keeps wandering and my body keeps craving till my skin feels like it's crawling.

I hug my sister and she promises we'll catch up soon. At

least she's forgiven me and I have her back on my side again. Sometimes doing what we think is the right thing isn't actually the right thing. I think we've both learned that lesson.

As I walk towards my car, Wolf pulls up and blocks my way.

"Look what the cat dragged in." He opens the door and swaggers towards me, a smirk on his face.

"Red seems to think my cat is dead."

"Explains the smell."

"That would be your scented candles all over the bath. You've gone soft."

"Your sister doesn't seem to think so."

I cringe and his smirk widens. "She's never been that smart."

"Must run in the family."

"At least we're pretty."

"Your sister is. You look like you cut your hair yourself, while blindfolded."

"It's called style, you should try it sometimes."

"Whatever helps you sleep at night."

"Who says I sleep at night?"

"Well, you sure as shit ain't getting laid."

I grind my teeth at his comment and his lips twitch. He's hit the jackpot, but he's also my best mate and knows that he can dig at me later. I have no doubt he will.

"You doing ok?" The smirk falls away and the amusement in his face evaporates.

I nod. I'm not. I'm sure Red will fill him in and I can have that conversation with him later.

"Good, then invest in a better fucking barber."

"Stop buying so many scented candles." I start walking away then stop and swivel back. "Hey, can I ask you a question?"

"Sure. You can ask, whether you'll get an answer is another matter."

I roll my eyes at him and his smirk is back. I make a mental note to text Red some shit about him later and let her deal with him. "How did you know?"

"Know what?"

"That Red was it?"

I can see thoughts flutter around his head as he considers giving me shit, but thinks better of it. He shrugs, looks at the house then back to me, "Guess she was just the right shade."

"What the fuck does that mean?"

He ignores me and makes his way to his door. I guess our conversation is over.

A Daryl Dark song belts out the radio, and I'm loath to listen to it and yet it draws me in. I know the lyrics and I watched this song being created and crafted. It's strange to have it drift through my car now. It forces my mind to go places I don't want to go. Everywhere I go she haunts me. The song ends and I find myself sighing before the DJ goes on about tickets going up for sale to Daryl's upcoming tour. It's going to sell out in hours. The man blathers on and then I stumble over his words. A new opening act, an up-and-coming talent in the rock world that's about to shake its foundations. Miss Emilia Stark. My heart seizes at the mention of the name. My heart ticks like it's counting seconds. I shake my head. Can't be.

The light turns red and I come to a stop, the idle engine purrs beneath me. There's a man walking on the pavement, wearing a black beanie and torn oversized jeans. A cigarette hangs from his mouth. He's carrying a big white bucket and a giant brush that looks more like a broom. He dips his brush into the bucket, smears the wall, then sticks up a poster on the already thick layers of aging, disintegrating paper and covers it with more glue before taking a sidestep and repeating the action.

The posters advertise Daryl's 'Drowning in Darkness' tour, but that's not what has me staring. It's the opening act. Emilia Stark and that's how she looks as she stares back at me from the poster. Dark eyeshadow and smokey eyes that make her look anything but shy and soft like I know she is.

I take a minute piecing things together. Fuck, maybe Wolf had a point and I am a bit slow. Horns blare and I realise the traffic light has changed to green. I take off.

Finally.

I've found her.

⸻

I drive straight to the office ignoring the questioning look I get from Rob. Why the hell is the guy always here? I glare back, his eyes dart away and fix on his screen. Good.

I crash into my chair and turn on my monitor, my leg tapping the floor as the computer comes to life.

I start with the socials. Emilia Stark is everywhere, profiles that were set up months ago. She looks fucking beautiful. Pictures of her in a studio, clips of her singing, glimpses of her when she isn't looking at the camera, capturing the depth she carries behind her eyes. All her socials are professional, none of my online tools find a personal profile.

I search Google. Hundreds of websites pop up. Suddenly she's everywhere. I read through the first four. They all have the same version of the same story. Unknown origins, endorsed by Daryl Dark, propelled to greatness. The new debut single is to be released on Friday. The album cover strikes me.

The title, spelt in big icy letters, jumps out. "Unrequited" stares at me and I stare back before taking in the other subtle details. An animated heart lays almost pulverised on a sea of shattered glass. It's a haunting image, I can almost feel that heart try to beat as it lays broken and dying. Beneath the glass written as if in marker with a rushed hand are the words "I wish you could have let go and fallen. It would have been an incredible adventure." I stare at the cover for a few minutes, taking everything in. For some reason, it feels as though it's talking to me.

I shrug it off and click back to the main search page and skim a few more articles. This is going to take all day.

I'm two hours in and bored of copy-pasted articles that give me no new information. I'm bombarded with pictures of her. Her face taunts me as it leers at me from across the screen. I'm still no closer to finding her now than I was two hours ago. I'm about to call every favour I am owed from every rich and arrogant person I've ever worked for when something catches my eye.

An obscure fan site that's only a week or so old. Poorly constructed and much of the same information, except for one glaring sentence that has my jaw finding the floor. I read over the words a few times like my mind can't compute eight simple words.

"Beloved daughter of legendary rock star Justin Legend."

I stare at the screen for a while. The shock drips through me like it's been hooked into my veins. "That son of a bitch." I whisper and grab my phone dialling his number.

He picks up after the third ring "Hunter."

I can hear the smile in his voice, I'm about to wipe it away, just like I do when I'm around his fucking daughter. "You should have told me."

"My daughter and I have a complicated relationship."

"You fucked your best friend's wife and left her pregnant to raise a kid alone?"

"Watch yourself, Hunter, we're not friends!" I'm guessing the smile is gone.

I bite my tongue and wait. He's right of course, but I'm angry and I want to find Emily.

He's silent for a long time, "I've tried to make amends."

I scoff. "You still should have told me."

"What can I do for you, Hunter? I'm a busy man." He's dismissive and flippant and I'm the help. He doesn't owe me an explanation.

"Is she the real reason you wanted me there?"

He remains silent.

His non-answer irks me, but I have more pressing things to deal with now. "I want to see her."

"Well, she's made it clear she doesn't want to see you." He doesn't sound like a rocker or a businessman anymore, he sounds like someone's father that's willing to do whatever it takes to protect his little girl. My heart pangs. What if her baby, *our* baby, is a girl?

I grind my teeth. "I need to talk to her."

"Hunter, you've been good to me over the years, and I have returned the gesture, but you're about to cross a line there is no coming back from."

I bite the inside of my cheek holding back an array of swearwords and insults I have prepared for this man. I inhale, swallowing them and pushing them down, "You owe me a favour."

"She's off limits."

"No. I want three backstage passes to the opening gig for Mr Dark's new tour."

"Hunter…" his voice carries a warning.

"You owe me. I just want to enjoy the show."

He scoffs. I've done Justin's personal protection many times over the last ten years, he is the king of loopholes, I know he appreciates mine.

"Should I inform our mutual friend about these tickets?"

"No."

"Are you sure this is the favour you want? You know you can have so much more."

"Just the tickets."

"I'll have my PA mail them to you."

"Thanks."

"And Hunter?"

"Yes sir?"

"I haven't been there for her much and our relationship is strained. But she's still my daughter and if you break her heart, I will find a way to end you. I have bigger friends than you"

"You can try," I smirk and hang up and think about the piles of dirt I have on all of them.

1 7

Hunter

Now that I know where she is, I see her everywhere. She follows me in the streets, on my phone, on my TV. She invades my car with her voice, and even my dreams aren't free of her. Except that in them, she's naked and in my arms and the sounds that she makes are only for me. I rip them from her red lips and own them.

I wake up sweating and painfully hard. My gaze falls onto the calendar as it has every morning for the last four months. Just two weeks to go till I see her. The last few months have been excruciating. Having her so out of reach is like a slow and painful death. Like I've been left to bleed out, but the cut is so small it leaks out in tiny droplets that weaken me but never run out.

I grab my phone, needing a distraction. Unable to find one. I'm irked by her—how she's managed to flip my whole carefully constructed life upside down. I'm doing shit I've never done before. I'm turning down offers for sex and killing myself at work so I won't have to think about her, just to have her song play at full volume and taunt me.

But more than that, I find myself entertaining a future I shouldn't want, with a family I don't even have. I get stupidly excited about it, about all the ifs. I'd take them for trips to the countryside and picnics in the park, and the movies and whatever else families do. I want this kid to have everything I didn't. But mostly love, cause they'd deserve that. I shut my eyes and push the thoughts away again. My feelings tangle in a wiry ball that tightens every time I try to unravel it.

And now? I'm trying to find some grand-fucking-gesture in way of apology, and I'm back on LyricsIncognito.com searching for original song lyrics. I want to surprise her. Getting those other lyrics made her so happy.

I input my usual search when something comes up. Original lyrics with handwritten notes, corrections, and connotations by one of her favourite artists. I remember how she went on about him one night. It was cute but annoying at the same time. I loved her passion, but man, it almost felt like she'd rather be there fucking him instead.

I look at the already inflated price. Four bidders pushing up the cost. I place a bid that should let them know I'm serious then set the phone down and get in the shower.

When I get back, I'm outbid. But not by much. I raise the price by five hundred quid and smirk to myself. No way anyone is getting those notes but me.

***

The night drags on. More overdressed, over-made-up girls getting drunk and sucking cock in the bathroom in the pursuit of love. Sometimes I wonder if desperation makes them think a way to a man's heart is through his cock.

I shrug it off and cover for Rob as he asks for a code 22. Seems like he spends most of the night getting off with some girl. I guess with Wolf being off the market and my recent mood, he's reaping the benefits.

I check my phone again; the bidder upped the bid by another thousand quid. They are not fucking around. I grind my teeth and think about the lump of money Legend sent me for babysitting Daryl. Guilt money. I was going to use it to buy a second property. Fuck it. Money comes and goes, and Legend will throw more my way in time. I raise by a single pound. I don't have to make big bids; I just have to win.

When I check again later, the bidder upped the bid by another grand. They're obviously not playing and think they can win. They won't. I look at the auction time, five minutes. I call Rob and ask him to take over. He approaches with a smirk on his face and pulls up his fly.

I hurry outside through the back door. Sam gives me a sideways look, seeing I stepped outside alone. I ignore him and keep walking. The door closes behind me and all that's left is the muted beat that thumps through the bricks. I lean against them. The cold air stings my face as I stare at the countdown clock. I know I'm not the only one watching, but I have to be careful, slow, and subtle. If I pounce too soon, I'll lose. I watch the seconds fall away, big red numbers that count down. With five seconds to go I input my last bid and hold my breath. The clock stops at zero and I keep watching the screen for confirmation.

I won. "Fuck yeah." I pump my fist in the air like an idiot then correct and look around making sure no one saw me. As I'm about to head inside, my screen flashes. It's a message from the other buyer.

'**Are you open to negotiating the sale of this item?**'

'**No.**' I type back and shake my head.

'**I'll pay you twice what you paid for it.**'

I sigh. '**It's not for sale.**'

'**Everything is for sale.**'

I ignore the message and tuck the phone back into my pocket. Not everything is. I have a stupid grin on my face for the rest of the night.

18

Hunter

ater. I keep reminding myself. I will have to wait till later to wipe the smirk off Wolf's face. He looks way too fucking pleased with himself watching me sweat like an idiot. Red is being reassuring and supportive, and as much as I love my sister, I wish she'd just shut the fuck up. I watch the raindrops as they race down the window and puddles form on the dark road as we race ahead.

The drive to Liverpool has already felt like three lifetimes, especially with these two. The minute I shut the door behind me, I regretted letting Red talk me into carpooling with them. She spends almost the entire trip telling me what a fuck up I am and how this is my chance to rectify things, while Wolf keeps asking if I need a nap or some sweeties like the overgrown asshat he is. All the pair of them did was get me more revved up. My body feels like a ticking bomb. Every muscle tight and twisted, my blood surging through my veins, burning me up from the inside, and it's all I can do to keep breathing through this nervous anticipation before I implode.

As soon as Wolf parks, I'm out of the car leaving them in my wake. They have their tickets, they'll catch up. I hear Red calling out to me and Wolf telling her to let me be. Raindrops fall on my head and slide down my face, cooling me down. With each step, they soak their way into my clothes till my shoulders feel damp and my pale blue jeans deepen to a darker hue. Typical weather in Liverpool.

I plough my way through the parking area and make my way to the back entrance. I know it's not where I'm meant to come in but old habits die hard and I don't give a shit. I just want to get inside so I can breathe and get away from this rain.

The usual die-hard groupies that hope to be allowed inside huddle like a bunch of soaked penguins. The rain lashes at them but they are tragic desperados. I never did get their obsession of wanting to rub shoulders with these guys. Maybe they think some of their shine will rub off. What they don't realise is that more often than not, it's just a bunch of shit tinted in gold and glitter.

The security guard gives me a sideways glance. He's young and fresh but he knows who I am. Everyone knows who I am. He checks my ticket and I step a little closer using my size to remind him where he ranks in the ladder. I'm broader, taller and I know my face mimics my insides— tense, angry, and impatient. He steps aside, letting me in.

The long white corridor leads to the backstage area. Awareness sheets my skin and chaos blooms in my chest. I know she's here somewhere, but I don't want to confront her before the show. I find a place in the shadows where I have a perfect vantage point to the stage but can't be seen.

The place is full, it's churning with fans. Most are here to see Daryl, at least that's what they think. They scream and clap and cheer. Their excitement fuels my impatience. Where the fuck is she?

The lights on the stage fade till darkness settles and the crowd loses it. The roar makes my bones vibrate and the walls shake with their voices. When I spot her, my heart stutters, and I suck in a sharp breath. She's wearing worn, faded jeans that mould to her perfect legs and are torn at the knees and upper thighs. Her black singlet rides up a little, revealing a slither of her perfectly flat stomach. My own churns and questions—which I've had for so long—slam inside me demanding answers. A black choker wraps around her delicate neck and my eyes keep getting drawn to it, missing all the places I once kissed and bit and licked. Her smokey eyes look out onto the crowd and her mouth stretches in a beautiful smile. My body ignites, an inferno of want fueled by confusion. A lethal combination.

The first notes of her song resonate through the arena and the crowd cheers like wild animals. Her voice carries across the human mass spread below her, and they answer her—word for word they sing her song and fill the arena with her music. The melody is as haunting as the lyrics and watching her wrench each word from her mouth, I'm surer than ever she wrote it for me. I can feel the agony she feels. It's written in the way her body moves and the way her voice stutters just beneath the surface, and I bet if I get any closer, her eyes would be glistening with unshed tears because she feels each syllable and note like a dagger. It all resonates inside her because she believes—she believes her love is unrequited.

And why wouldn't she? I've never given her a reason to think otherwise.

The song draws to an end and my heart is a twisted, crumpled mess as the crowd erupts into another burst of clapping. She's broken and elated, and it takes everything inside of me not to run onto that stage and pull her into my arms, not to confess everything. I will. Later. First, she gets to have her moment. She gets to make her dream come true. To be Emilia Stark and not Emilia Legend. She's built her own empire by climbing over everyone else's shit. A burst of heat moves through my chest as I watch her own her dreams.

***

Sweat covers her face and a droplet rolls down her back, but she's all smiles as she leaves the stage. The crowd is a monster of sound, clapping and chanting her name. I can't blame them. She is a goddess, and like them, I'm here to worship her.

I step out of my hiding place. Wolf who's been standing with his arm around my sister on the wing, spots me and falls in just behind. Maybe he senses the chaos I'm about to unleash. He's good like that, Wolf. I know no matter what he always has my back.

I'm right behind her group. They all talk in rushed sentences, too loud and too animated. Adrenaline still coursing through them. She's giddy, laughing with her guitarist. He has a hand around her shoulder as they walk through the corridor, and I make a mental note to break every bone in his hand. *Later.*

"Emily," I call for her and she swivels around. Her eyes grow wide and her mouth falls slightly open, the beautiful smile vanishes. I guess I'm back to having that effect on her. Her brow furrows and then without a word she turns back around and keeps walking down the corridor.

"Emily," I say again, picking up speed.

"Go away," she calls over her shoulder and doesn't stop. She's approaching a crowd. Three security guards stand at the door holding them back. They're calling her name and holding up posters and t-shirts for her to sign. They probably won some kind of competition to get to spend some time with her after the concert.

I'm about to disappoint a whole bunch of people. Lucky I don't give a shit.

"We need to talk," I call over her bandmates, who all slow down and start looking between me and her.

"No, we don't." She still won't stop.

"Who is this guy?" The guitarist asks her as his hand closes around her again.

Brave.

I'll give him that. Also incredibly stupid.

"No one," she says as she closes the distance to the crowd. Once she reaches them. It'll be more difficult.

No one?

I bulldoze through her band members ignoring their calls of "hey" and "what the hell?" and grab her elbow. The three burly security guys turn to look at me as I start pulling her away. I need her calm enough so we can get through the crowd without incident.

Emily is talking to me *today*. Now! Whether she wants to or not. I deserve answers and she needs to know... everything.

"Let go of me," she calls out, and all eyes in the room fall on my hand locked on her elbow. In a second the band members dash out of the way, all except the guitarist. The three security guys make a move towards us. They're a little smaller than me, definitely younger which means they lack experience. But I have one thing that those guys never will. A Wolf.

Emily's eyes grow wide, and I can see in the mirror behind her Wolf has his hand on her guitarist, explaining that if he ever wanted to play again, he best walk away.

He steps in front of me and blocks the advancing security team. "Go. I'll sort out these guys." He's already got a plan and I see them hesitate. I know there's no chance anyone will stop us now.

I pull her along as she struggles and screams and tries to pull out of my grip. "If you don't stop fighting, I'm going to throw you over my shoulder and carry you out of here in front of all your fans."

"Fuck you, Hunter! Let me go, now!"

"Final warning," I say as she pulls and tries to yank herself away.

"Hunt—" the rest of my name is a garbled scream as I pick her up, haul her over my shoulder and push my way through the few who still stand in my way. Most have their phones out filming. If Wolf and the other boys know what they are doing, that footage will disappear. A few of the fans scream at me, but no one plays the hero.

I chance a quick glance over my shoulder. Wolf is talking the other guys down and remains ever the professional, it's another reminder of how much things have changed. In the past, we would have stood and fought all of them—and won —then gone to a bar for a beer and laughed before taking a groupie or two home.

Now, he has to think about my sister too—who is some-where behind us—and I have shit to sort out with Emily. How things have changed.

***

Her dressing room is a few steps from the crowd. I rip open the door, kicking it shut behind me before I fling her on the sofa inside and slide in beside her.

"What the hell Hunter?" She screams in my face and tries to slap me. I catch her hand and throw it away.

Someone clears their throat and I turn to find Emily's PA standing by the mirror clutching a folder of some kind. He's tall and skinny and all the colour has drained from his face.

"Take off," I growl at him. He looks at Emily, uncertainty plastered across his pale face. She's rubbing her elbow and her eyes are alight.

"Miss?"

"Stay where you are, he's leaving," she hisses.

Fuck it. I throw down the gauntlet, if she wants to do this in front of an audience that's her choice. Either way, we're talking. I don't exactly know where to start, my heart hammers in my chest and there is a roaring inside my head that won't relent. "Your song, Unrequited, is that about me?"

"You? It has nothing to do with you. Get out of my dressing room."

"No, answer me." Her eyes dart over to her PA. That guy needs to go. "You! Give us some privacy."

"Ignore him, George, he's leaving now."

"Answer me."

"Get out!"

"Miss, do you need a hand?" The P.A. shifts uncomfortably where he stands. He knows a fight with me will not end well for him.

"She's fine," I assure him.

"Hunter!"

"Was it?"

"Miss."

"Emily!"

She crushes me with a hot look before defeat paints her face. "It's fine George, thanks. Give us a minute will you?"

The P.A. stares at me for another second before nodding and rushing out of the room and we're alone. Rain beats at the window and thunder claps somewhere in the distance.

Emily faces me and sighs, "What do you want Hunter?"

"Answers. Like where the hell have you been? And why are you avoiding me? And that fucking song, Emily. I need answers."

She nods and settles back into her seat.

There's a commotion outside, shouting and screaming. I guess Wolf is reassuring the response team that there is nothing to see here. Took them way too long to get back here. I make a mental note to speak to her about her security detail. This bullshit will not stand. But that's a problem for later. The noise mutes, just the lashing of the rain against the building.

"Is that what you came all this way to ask me? About the song?"

I grind my teeth, "Answer me. Is it about me? Us?"

Her teeth drag along her lower lip which tips down, "How could it be about you when you've never been in love?"

"Who said I've never been in love?"

"You!" She sticks her finger out and shoves my chest. "You told me it was a transient, chemical reaction in the brain, just a meaningless word that will never be real for you."

"I was an idiot."

"Was?"

"Look, I saw the test." I blurt out. My eyes dart from her face to her stomach.

"Is that the real reason you're here?"

I shake my head. Confusion reigns inside my head, all logical thought lost to the chaos inside. "I have the right to know."

She looks down at her belly and her hands skate over the perfectly flat surface. "You weren't meant to see it."

"But I did." Her eyes collide with mine, glistening with unshed tears.

She nods.

"Was it mine? Ours? Did you lose…" I swallow, "it?"

She shakes her head, and her eyes fall away from mine. "No. I mean yes, but no."

"Emily, I don't under—"

"It would have been ours."

"Would have been?"

"False-positive. I had a blood test."

I feel simultaneously relieved and wistful. Somewhere inside of me, I had accepted that I might be a father, that a part of me was growing inside of her, and a future I'd never imagined was possible. I didn't realise how much I had fallen in love with the idea until just now when it's been snatched away.

"Oh." Is all I can manage. There will be time later to sift through all my feelings. There are just too many now for me to deal with. "Are you ok?"

"I am now. It was confusing."

I nod unsure if I should draw her into me. If she wants me to. My hands fist the sofa and dig into the fabric.

"I was scared and thought I was alone. When the blood tests came back negative, I was devastated because I didn't realise I already loved this baby that never existed, so much. But I was also relieved because you didn't..." she sighs

We sit in a swollen silence for a while. Only the rain, a witness to our misery and loss.

"You didn't answer any of my calls..."

"I was hurt and angry and you made it clear you didn't want to be trapped. Then I took the test..."

"I didn't think I wanted any of those things. My job is not exactly conducive to relationships..."

"You think too much."

"Maybe..."

"Maybe?" she scoffs and her mouth downturns, making my heart tighten in my chest. "Your head is too full of strategies and boundaries and denial; you want to control everything, and you are so stubborn you can't let anything go. When you understand that you need to think less and feel more, you might realise that a heart, unlike the mind, is always honest. At all costs. Which is why it's so scary, which is why it gets exposed and vulnerable. Which is why it hurts so badly when it knows the one it wants doesn't want it back."

"Emily—"

"It's fine. I'd rather you were honest, and I don't need a placeholder till the "real thing" comes along. I deserve more."

"You do."

She purses her lips as if there's no more left to say.

"You were right though," Her eyes lift and look at me growing wide, "I am a coward, and I should have never made you feel like I was your placeholder when you were my everything."

The silence lays like honey between us, sweet and sticky and hard to navigate through. Emily stands up and finds her reflection in the mirror. Some of her makeup has smudged with tears and sweat, but she still looks stunning. She leans over the chair and catches my eyes in her reflection. When she shakes her head, her whole face falls, and I feel the stab of her words before they come.

"I don't think you mean that. You only think you love me because of the baby you thought we were going to have. You don't owe me anything."

The pain in my chest intensifies like drowning. It's hard to breathe and everything burns and hurts. I bolt from the sofa and advance on Emily. My body craves her, I crave her; but first, she has to hear everything I have to say. My hands rest on the chair, caging her in. I hold my body at bay, knowing I'm an impulse away from doing something stupid.

"You piss me off." I start and maybe they're the wrong words to say, but they are true. "Everything about you gets my blood boiling."

She tries to push away from me, but I pin her to the chair with my body. Heat rushes through me, but it has to wait. I find her eyes and hold them with my own. "I get all riled about stupid shit that shouldn't even matter and for reasons I can't explain. *Couldn't* explain."

I take a sharp breath, "It pissed me off when you laugh with other people because I want to be the guy making you laugh, and it pisses me off when you dress up to go out cause I want to be the guy who gets to take you out, and it pisses me off when you have conversations with other people and I can't contribute and impress you with my charm and intelligence." That gets me a quirky smile and I keep going.

"It pisses me off when I wake up in the morning and you're not there with me, and it pisses me off that I haven't kissed you, or seen you, or talked to you in six long, excruciating months cause all I want is to stop being pissed off and just be happy—with you. You make me happy, Emily. Being with you, around you, sharing things with you, it makes me happy and I've been miserable without you."

My heart ricochets against my ribs, and I hold my breath for a second before releasing it, "I love you, Emilia."

Her eyes glisten and she pushes against my chest again. This time I let her and step back, she slides away from me and her eyes snap to mine, "You can't just say that now."

"I mean it."

"I just—"

"Wait," I forestall her with a wave of my hand and reach into my jeans where her present has been tucked uncomfortably into my pants, "I got you something."

Her eyes shoot up and she gives me a quizzical look as I hand her the parcel.

She takes it tentatively and undoes the silver bow holding it together. The lyrics are meticulous, scribbled with the author's handwriting and other delicate markings. A composition. A confession of his soul's greatest secrets on paper. She gasps and her eyes grow bigger as she looks through the pages.

Her eyes dart to mine for a second before they go back to the pages. I think that I've rendered her speechless, which makes me both insanely happy and uncomfortable.

"It was you?"

"Me?"

"You were the second bidder?"

Oh. I shrug.

"You ignored my messages." She smacks my arm.

"As I said, it wasn't for sale and no amount of money would have been enough."

She makes a tiny sound and hugs the pages to her chest, "I wanted these so much you have no idea—" The caramel of her eyes swirls and melts and before I grasp what's happening, she's closed the distance between us and pushed up onto her tiptoes. Her lips slam into mine, her hands thread through my hair, and my body comes alive for her like it always does. She tastes better than I remember, and as I wrap my hands around her, I know I'm not letting go—not until my body is done telling her anything my words haven't been able to.

Twisting her hair around my fist I tug, pulling her head up, deepening our kiss. I forgot how exquisite she is, and I'm going to take my time reminding myself. Except that there's a pounding at the door, and a man calls out her name. The door is still closed, so I know Wolf still has the situation under control. But maybe until they see her safe, we won't get to be alone.

She pulls away from me, her heated eyes on mine, her rapid breath searing my skin. "I better—"

"Yeah." I give her a quick peck before I begrudgingly release her.

She opens the door. Wolf is there blocking it with his oversized frame while two of the three security guards bounce up and down in front of him, their faces set somewhere between fear and anger. The relief is instantaneous but brief, as they hurl questions at her. She assures them she is fine and when she asks Wolf to step out of the way, they want to charge into the room to face me. They weigh up the odds of the two of them against the two of us and keep asking Emily if she is ok, if she feels safe or requires assistance.

When she reassures them enough, they glare at Wolf and me a few more times before leaving the room.

Emily's eyes flash between Wolf, Red and me who all stand huddled by the doorway.

"Thanks," I say to Wolf and Red hoping they know how much I appreciate the time they bought me, but also that they now need to leave me with my girl so I can keep explaining how I feel. Naked.

"Sure thing," Wolf's smug face splits with a grin, "is it my turn with her now then?"

Without missing a beat Emily looks into his big eyes and asks, "Are you talking to him or me?" While Red elbows him in the ribs. He recoils and bursts out laughing, I glare at my best mate while holding back my own laughter. I don't even have to say anything, Red will punish him later. The thought forces the smile on my face, and it's Emily who elbows me next.

"Oi, what did I do?"

She giggles as she and Red exchange a look.

"I'm Emilia, but my friends call me Emily."

Red smiles at her, "Red, I'm this idiot's sister." Her head tips in my direction.

Emily nods, "He's told me about you."

"All lies I'm sure."

"Probably." They laugh at my expense and Wolf's grin just keeps getting wider. I'll deal with him later.

"So... thanks for your help," I say again, flicking my eyes and tipping my head towards the door. They all ignore me as Red and Emily keep talking and Wolf is seconds away from bursting into full-on laughter as he keeps his eyes on me and my growing frustration. We both know all he has to do is put his hand over Red's shoulder and lead her out of the room, but he doesn't. He's enjoying this way too much. I suck in a deep breath and calm myself with all the ways I'm going to hurt him.

Somewhere in the building a boom echoes. Daryl must have finally taken the stage.

Red turns to Wolf and he nods, his face softening. She turns back to Emily, "I'm going to go watch the show, it was nice meeting you."

She pulls her into an embrace, and I see her lips moving while she whispers into her ear. Emily nods and gives her a beautiful, shy smile as she releases her.

Red and Wolf finally leave the room and I stalk Emily. She backs up till her back hits the wall and I'm on her in a second. Finally, I can have her. Except that there's another knock on the door and I rip my lips from hers, "What?"

The PA is back, he looks flustered. He bounces slightly on his toes and he's chewing his lip like it's a piece of gum. His eyes flash from me to Emily and back to me. "What?" I growl at him, and he turns his attention back to his boss,

"I'm so sorry Miss Stark, but the fans have been waiting. It's in your contract that you have to—"

I groan as Emily nods, "Give me five minutes George, I just want to fix my makeup."

Emily pushes me away and I roll along the wall, my head hitting the plaster with a thud as I stare at her ass. "Fuck," I groan again as Emily makes her way to the vanity and starts playing with her hair and makeup.

My body aches and my impatient cock twitches in my boxers.

When she is done she stands up and saunters over. She flattens me with a look before pushing up and kissing me lightly on the lips. "Don't go anywhere." She warns me before leaving the room and closing the door behind her.

———

Emily

I'm elated and exhausted. I didn't expect to have so many people hanging around wanting my signature. The adrenaline of the day begins to wear off, and I know Hunter is waiting for me in my dressing room. My body tingles thinking about him. I've missed him so much, missed his touch, missed the way his body makes mine feel.

But if he thinks he can just waltz in and erase all his words with some grand gesture and declaration of love, he's mistaken. Isn't he? My heart throbs and aches. I've been wanting this for so long, *him* for so long. But the hurt tinkers inside me, splintering the hope I want to build. What if all it is are words? Transient feelings? My heart will crumple. I don't know if I can help myself around him.

But then I think about the lyrics. He paid attention. He knew where to find them and he outbid me at a significant cost. He went out of his way, he wanted me to have something that I love. As much as I love him. He showed up. He's here and I'm the one who's given him endless speeches about vulnerability and taking chances, maybe it's time to take my own advice.

I walk into the room, and before I have a chance to say anything, I'm in his arms and his lips seal around mine, stealing my breath.

"What took you so long?" he growls, his hot breath skates over my neck followed by his tongue and teeth, leaving behind a heated trail of desire.

I lick my lips, my hands already buried in his hair. I don't know what took so long and I don't care, I've already forgotten about all those other people out there. They don't matter, only we matter.

His body pushes mine and leads me to the sofa lounged against the wall, where we fall in a heap.

"Fuck, I've missed you." His gruff voice sears my skin and need overwhelms me.

"I've missed you too," I whimper as he lays another kiss on my neck, his hands already tugging at my shirt. I let him rip it from my body and he throws it carelessly somewhere in the room.

"I'm going to remind you what you've been missing, and when I'm done, all your fans will know my name."

Heat singes my face and burns my ears, flooding my body with desire. "Hunter." He smiles at the mention of his name, tears at my clothes and pushes me onto the soft sofa. His eyes track my naked body as he rips off his shirt and pulls down his jeans and boxers in one movement, releasing his hard cock. I can't help but look, catching myself licking my lips. He is a masterpiece of strength and muscles.

He falls to his knees in front of me and painfully, slowly his graceful fingers trace my body, leaving behind blazing trails of want. Goosebumps erupted along my skin and my nipples harden, aching with need. His touch makes my skin feel alive like it's separate to the rest of me. I whimper as he touches everywhere but the places I want him most. A long torture that plays with my sanity.

"Hunter," I breathe out his name and he smirks. *All your fans will know my name.*

His mouth on my skin is like fire. The gentle kiss lands just above my right hip bone. I gasp at the sensation and have no time to think as the next one follows and then another. And I *feel* everything. Plump, warm lips, that I've missed so much that have learned my body and know what it needs.

He kisses every inch of my skin, avoiding the places that so desperately ache for him. Even when I arch he ignores me. Kissing my neck and tracing my collar bone with his tongue, nipping at my navel and my ankles till he rips my legs apart and kisses my inner thighs. His harsh bristles scratch my skin. Still, he skips over my aching pussy, and I groan, unravelling.

"Hunter…" I moan out his name, imploring. Begging.

He groans with the first lash of his tongue and my body jerks at the exquisite sensation. My body aches for him to have another. And he does.

His tongue swirls and circles my clit, and my fingers claw into his scalp. I feel his smile against my skin while his tongue continues to lavish my clit. He holds down my thighs, his fingers digging into me as my pleasure builds. Whimpers rip from my mouth as my body quivers and tightens. His hand creeps along my navel and up towards my breast, the sensation painfully good. I arch into his touch and the light stroke sets my body on fire, tipping me over the edge. Pleasure bleeds into every inch of me. I cry out as it rips through my body and washes over me. Hunter's tongue and hands tease and stoke and lick while I grind into him, until the very last wave.

His body crawls over mine slowly, leaving behind gentle kisses over my body. He takes a nipple into his mouth and groans, sending shivers across my body. He takes his time. His tongue, his lips, his teeth all pull and tug and taunt my aching nipples till tears gather in my eyes and a new ache builds between my legs.

"Please," I beg him, suffering through frustration,

He kisses his way up to my neck, "Did you miss me?" he whispers, his breath fanning my ear as he lays a kiss on my shoulder.

"Yes." My pulse drums against my throat a second before his lips brush over my own. His tongue touches the seam of my lips and vanishes, leaving behind a whisper of a taste. My taste.

He pulls me off the couch and puts me on my knees, then nudges my head onto the sofa. He leans forward, his large body caging mine. The hair on his chest tickles my skin. His hands cord around me like chains drawing me to him, moulding me to him like we're one. I know this is where I belong, in his arms. It's where I've always belonged.

One of his hands slips between my thighs, ripping a moan from my mouth. I grind against the pressure of his fingers on my clit. My need for him is a hungry craving. He feels it. He knows what I want.

I expect it, and yet I whimper when his fingers slide into me. So easily. His fingers swirl and his hard cock digs into my ass as he presses against me making sure I know how hard he is.

"I've missed you too, Emily." His husky voice rumbles in my ear as his fingers circle my clit ever so slowly teasing, leaking tension into my body instead of relief.

Before I have a chance to respond, he lines up his cock and slams into me. I cry out. The line between pleasure and pain, a thin, delicious blur. He stills inside me for a beat, his chest expands with his sharp intake of breath and a low growl which makes my heart kick up.

My body trembles, his unrelenting fingers circle my clit and his cock ploughs into me. He assumes all my senses, weakening me, breaking me, tormenting me, making me his with every second. I drown in him.

He steals my breath with every move, with every swivel of his fingers, every thrust of his cock. A hungry desire to fall over the precipice grips me. He's unrelenting, ravaging me. Marking me. Reminding me of everything I've missed.

Hunter sets a brutal pace. I can't help but push back to meet his thrusts. I moan for him, meeting him thrust for thrust, needing all of him deeper harder. He makes me burn. I moan for him as my orgasm builds, my head falls against his hard chest.

"Fuck Emily." His thrusts are erratic now, his fingers stroke my clit. My senses reel and my breath halts as my vision darkens. The edge has never felt so sharp, so steep.

And then with a final brutal slam, my orgasm smashes me to pieces. "Hunter," I call out his name as I cum, and my pussy grinds against him as he jerks inside me, burying himself deeper as I squeeze around him.

He holds me till the last shudders fall away and my erratic breathing settles and my body feels like it might belong to me again, like gravity has remembered to pull it back down.

"Hunter." My voice sounds foreign, wrecked and needy.

"I love you." His raspy voice sends a shiver down my spine, his hot breath fanning the crock of my neck. My heart chugs and emotion clogs my throat.

EPILOGUE

SIX MONTHS LATER

Hunter

The doorbell rings and Emily shrieks, "They're here."

I can't help but smile as she runs out of the room. I look around at our suitcases, they line the floor like a deformed caterpillar. Two are mine, the rest are hers. Daryl's world tour kicks off next week, and with her success during all his UK gigs, he's taking her along for the ride.

Of course, she needed her own personal bodyguard and who better than me? I'm going to guard her body with my life, keeping it close. My cock jerks to life as I start to imagine all the ways her body will need protecting —from me.

My thoughts are interrupted by the voices downstairs. I sigh, adjust, and head down.

Red looks lovely and is hanging off Emily, who is smiling at her. They are thick as thieves, and this both delights and scares me. My sister's best friend should not be the woman I'm in love with and roll around naked with. Wolf hangs back, checking out Red's ass. I hate when he does that, but it's also reassuring that he only has eyes for her. I know he'll never hurt her.

I exchange a hello with them, already wishing they would leave so I can spend the night with Emily, keeping her close and naked. My body craves her like a parched man covets a drink.

I follow them outside where a table is set for the four of us by the pool. Candles float in the water, shimmering on the surface. A light breeze cools the humid air.

"Are you all set for tomorrow?" Red asks as she takes her seat between Emily and Wolf.

"Yeah, I'm petrified."

"You're going to kill it."

"Thanks." Emily blushes and the pink tint on her cheeks makes my cock jerk. I love that side of her, those shy nuances she throws out into the world, and only I get to see it when she unravels. "I'm just sorry I won't be around for your show."

"It's ok. If this one goes well, there will be plenty of others."

"If?" Wolf raises an eyebrow. "When," He states it like it's a fact and his hand slithers onto my sister's thigh before he leans in and kisses her. I've learned to live with his affection towards her. At least he's learned to tone it down when I'm around. I clear my throat and he reluctantly pulls away from her before winking at me. I grind my teeth, adding yet another transgression to the endless list Wolf will have to pay for. But not tonight. Tonight we celebrate.

We eat and laugh and talk and drink. For the first time in my life, I feel complete. I feel like I have something that's bigger than me. I'm not skirting the edges, but I'm part of a whole that surrounds me. I have a family and I have love and I'm so fucking happy.

The girls go off into the house, Red wants to see something of Emily's and we promised to clear the table while they're gone.

When they disappear into the house, Wolf turns to me. "I have something for you."

"You? For me?"

"Yeah." His face remains serious, "Trust me, you're going to need this."

"Trust you?" I quirk an eyebrow as he pulls something out and hands it to me. It's wrapped delicately in golden paper and a sweet bow. The more I study it, the more suspicious I grow. Wolf keeps his face schooled and neutral, which tells me he is battling hard not to laugh.

"Thanks." I set it down on the table and watch his face collapse a little.

"You should open it.'

"I will." I grab my beer and take a sip watching him twitch.

His eyes keep darting from me to the gift that lies between us, then he shrugs and grabs his own beer like he can't be fucked what I do. I know he is bothered, but his reaction gets under my skin like he knew it would. The man is an asshole.

I grip the gift and his lips twitch in a victory smile.

Fuck it, let's get this over with.

I unwrap the present, and as I do, Wolf can no longer contain himself and his smile gets wider and wider as he eyes me ripping through the paper.

I look from Wolf to the gift then back to Wolf, who is barking out laughter. "Told you you'll need it." He chocks through bouts of laughter.

I look at the scented candle in my hand—vanilla and sandalwood. Emily would probably like it, but Wolf can't know that.

"Yeah no thanks, I'm not going to go soft like you." I chuck it in his direction and he ducks, the candle missing his head by inches. It clatters on the wooden patio and I hear the plop as it disappears in the pool.

"What the fuck man? That's not how you say thank you for a thoughtful gift."

"Thoughtful, my ass."

"I think you need to go retrieve it and then say thank you."

"I think you can go fuck yourself."

In a second we are out of our chairs and onto each other. Adrenaline courses through me as we tangle and wrestle with one another. It feels so familiar, and even as we push and shove and grapple for a dominant position, I realise how fucking happy I am.

We get nearer to the pool as we push and shove, neither of us is really hitting hard. We won't hurt each other, but there's no way either of us is losing. The girls walk out to find us mid-wrestle.

"What are you doing?" Emily's mouth falls open and she looks worried, while Red rolls her eyes and shakes her head.

"Just let the children work it out."

Blood rushed to all my muscles and our egos battle just as much as our bodies. Wolf smirks as he tries to get out of my clinch. We shuffle back and forth, locked in a grappling hold when we both make a move to disconnect and regain posi- tion. The action sends us to the edge of the pool where Wolf loses his balance. His hand locks around my shirt and a second later I'm plunged into the cold water.

I resurface to see Red and Emily standing a few steps away. Wolf is by me and we're both howling with laughter.

Red takes a step closer and looks down at Wolf, "Well, get your ass out here. Now I'm going to have to get your big ass home and get you out of those wet clothes."

"Don't even pretend you don't want to," his eyebrows jump up and down, and Red giggles as vomit climbs up my throat.

"Oi, you mind?"

"Not at all." Wolf winks at me before pulling himself out of the pool and pushing my head back under in the process. Water drags off him in sheets, and he rushes my sister, grabbing her in his arms and soaking her through.

"For fuck sakes, Shaw."

"Guess we're both wet now." He grins at her wickedly and she shoves him, but nowhere near as hard as she should. Instead, she looks at him in a way I don't want to see.

Red turns to Emily, "Guess we better get out of here then."

Emily is red in the face, smiling, flustered and amused. "Can I get you guys some towels?"

"We're fine," Wolf says as he wraps himself around Red and shoves her with his body towards the door.

"I'll call you tomorrow," Red calls over her shoulder, "Thanks for dinner, good luck Em."

"Thanks." Emily looks after them and then swivels around, taking in the destruction. The table is still full of plates that are covered in food, two chairs have fallen over, and I'm in the pool, grinning at her.

"Are you two ever going to grow up?"

"What for?"

She stands above me shaking her head pretending she doesn't love this side of me.

"Help a guy out?" I stretch out and she reaches for my hand. I yank as hard as I can, her scream drowns out as she hits the water with a splash.

She resurfaces. Her hair plastered to her face, her make up running, her mouth set in an annoyed grimace. "What the hell, Hunter?"

I drag her hand, pulling her through the water and push her against the wall where I pin her down, our faces an inch apart, "It's better to ask for forgiveness than permission." I smirk and brush her lips with mine, the grimace dissolving away.

"You are pretty good at apologizing." A hint of a smile crosses her beautiful lips, and I kiss her. Hard. Because she's mine. The thought sets me alight.

"Well, there's nothing I'd like more than to spend the rest of tonight apologizing" I give her my most charming smile and feel her melt around me as my body burns for her.

I wrap my hands around her and draw her to me, my lips sealing around hers in a scorching kiss that promises all our desires will be fed. I love this woman so much; I know that all I want to do is to make her feel as happy as I do every single fucking day forever.

I've always been good at being someone else's something, but now all I want is to be her everything.

The End

If you enjoyed Hunter and Emily's story, please consider leaving a review on Amazon and Goodreads.

UNREQUITED

I have loved you in the dark, where all my secrets live
    Where you dragged my heart through broken glass
    And left me to starve, heartsick with the famine of
desire

You confined my love, forced it into helpless hiding
    Where it was doomed to swim in the murky
waters of your heart
    Where you couldn't see me, where you never
saw me

But even through my descent, a free fall into agony
    I will never regret you
    I will never forget you
    You've ruined me

I've fought to rip my desire for you from my bones
    To shatter my love into a million pieces of glass
    But they are everywhere I go, slicing into my skin

There is no way to recover from a love so strong or
fierce
    The exquisite pain loving you gave me is engraved
in my soul
    My broken heart bleeds salty tears that sting the
open wound

The joke's on me
    Have the last laugh
    I can't lose something that I never had
    So tell my heart
    To stop falling apart
    Cause even though it knows, it still hurts so bad

But even through my descent, a free fall into agony
    I will never regret you
    I will never forget you
    You've ruined me

ACKNOWLEDGMENTS

I would like to start by thanking you the reader, so much for reading! If you enjoyed the story, please leave a review and recommend the book to any friend you think would love this story. You will have my eternal love and gratitude.

A massive thank you to Tracey Caldwell, your input and encouragement has been amazing.

To K despite your still terrible taste in beverages, when you're not the worst you're the best, another book that wouldn't have made it to the shelf without you. You know how much your input, laughter and late nights mean to me. Thank you x.

ABOUT THE AUTHOR

Jane Wynters doesn't quite know how to answer the question of "where are you from?" She's moved from place to place like a snowflake on the wind always searching for a safe place to land. She loves meeting new people and exploring new places. She loves reading, writing and conjuring new worlds from her imagination. Coffee is at the top of her food pyramid and she is fluent in three languages and sarcasm.

Want to know more about the author and keep in touch? Get snippets of upcoming books and have a bit of twisted fun? Come join me in Wonderland…